GIRLS' NIGHT

THE GIRLS' TRILOGY
BOOK 2

JASON LETTS

1

"Alice... Alice!"

An insistent voice from the desk next to mine tears me away from my thoughts. No, I haven't already forgotten that I'm no longer Emily Marks, financial planner, and need to respond to the name of Alice Patterson, human resources officer, but I did think I'd be able to spend more than three minutes at work before someone tested me on it.

I twist gingerly considering the pain in my legs, hip, ribs, and neck. Oh, and of course my face too, which has a massive bruise on the left cheek that stretches from my ear and neck to my nose and mouth. It's a kaleidoscope of discomfort, dark red in the middle but yellow and purple starting to creep in around the edges.

The middle-aged lady with thick arms and a floral dress next to me, Janice according to the nameplate, does a double take when she notices my condition, averting her eyes then shifting back to gawk unabashedly.

In a way, it's disappointing. I put all this work into looking like Alice, wearing her conservative clothes and necklace, even going to the salon to get my hair the exact right shade and

soon as I tip my head, but all anyone is going to notice is this bruise.

I strain to make a smile even though it stings, causing my face to flare up.

"Good morning," I say, speaking slowly and more nasally as Alice did. "What can I help you with?"

When Janice cringes at me and recoils, I know I've done something wrong. She's got her guard up and is acting like I'm trying to trick her, and I can't figure out if it's because Alice is viciously manipulative or if Janice is figuring out that by posing as Alice I am in fact trying to trick her.

"You'll need to help yourself as much as you can," she says defensively then casts a sidelong glance at my bruise again. "The director wants to see you in his office in ten minutes."

My breath catches in my throat, and I wonder if I've been caught already. I'm kicking myself for how stupid I am to think I could waltz into work pretending to be a different person and expect to get away with it. For all I know, he has the McCurtain County sheriff in there with him ready to arrest me for making Taylor drive a kitchen knife into the heart of the real Alice.

I tell myself there's no way I've been caught already, not when I've only shown up to work moments ago and haven't been able to fully figure out what happened in Hochatown myself.

Playing it cool, I nod slightly to Janice, who keeps sneaking glances at me like she can tell something's wrong.

"Do you know what it's about?" I ask, giving her another excuse to look me over. I wonder if she can tell I'm a little thinner than Alice or that my eyes are a notch darker.

Janice leans back in her swivel chair and exhales forcefully. I have to twist my neck more to look back at her, making my skin feel like it's going to rip apart.

"I haven't ever been called into Director Zee's office," she

listening. "If he wants to see you, something is up."

I wheeze, suddenly petrified about what I'm in for. Could it be that Alice actually doesn't have the kind of job security I imagined? Maybe she was about to get fired and took a vacation with us anyway.

Or, more likely, maybe the director found out about Alice's weird plan to make people do her bidding. Taylor could be in there spilling the beans that she was forced into servitude while resigning over her own fraudulent résumé.

"Alright, thanks," I mutter to Janice, knowing even that is nicer than Alice could be.

I glance at the clock on the computer and wonder what I'm going to do until I need to comply with the summons, but the answer finds me instead of the other way around.

I used to have waking nightmares about the horrible things I've done, but since driving away from Hochatown I've been racking my brain trying to figure out exactly what happened. I'm left with countless questions that the little information I have can't begin to cover.

What happened to Wesley and Taylor after they left the cabin on Broken Bow Lake? I assumed they started running for it after what they did to Cletus and Alice, perhaps reuniting considering they'd been texting with each other and scheming for months before the trip to the lake, but I can't be sure.

What happened to the guy from the bar, who turned out to be a complete psycho? After I'd claimed to be a fellow victim instead of a perpetrator in the death of Alice, who I said was me, the sheriff said they'd call me with any news, but I haven't heard about an arrest of a one-eyed man. As far as I know, he could still be out there.

The biggest question of all is one only time can answer. Can I really pull off being Alice while she's locked in a morgue freezer?

wound, and it was Taylor's fingerprints, not mine, on the knife, but I wonder if I'll be spending the entire remainder of my life constantly worried someone will figure out I'm not who I say I am.

At least my parents are in prison and would celebrate the news of my death, happily embracing any suggestion I'm gone, while as best I can tell, Alice's parents haven't contacted her in four years and may never do so again.

But I close my eyes and think about how it all turned out this way, getting me to this moment. When I lied about the car not starting, I was facing complete destitution, the loss of my job, and the likelihood of having to scrape by as a thief and a cheat.

One of the last things my sister Melanie said to me before she died in a car accident was, "If you're going through hell, keep going!" All I knew was that I couldn't leave Hochatown beaten like I was, and my only option was to stick it out on the chance that it would get better.

I didn't know I would be the last one of us three standing, but that gamble paid off.

Glancing at the clock, I can see it's time for me to go, so I stiffly rise from my seat and try to stretch my aching joints.

Until I'm able to relax and feel like no one's going to question that I'm Alice, I know I'll have to keep finding a way forward, and right now that means faking it through this meeting with Bedrock Financial's human resources director.

Janice casts me another suspicious glance as I set off, and other human resources staff members subtly watch me pass through the office to the short hall where the director's office is.

I know being late won't help me, but I can't help dragging my feet as I try to map out as many possible scenarios as I can. If I see law enforcement, I'll run for it. If Director Zee suggests I'm not Alice, I'll blame it on my injuries.

hearing about the harrowing double murder at the lake. I'd be more than happy to put on a very sad face and commiserate about the loss of poor Emily Marks, a promising new financial planner whose résumé we definitely do not need to examine now that she's going to be pushing up daisies.

My breathing is ragged, and I'm having trouble hiding my limp as I reach the office, which the opaque glass door proclaims in large gold letters as being for Human Resources Director Ron Zee.

Sure my silhouette can be seen from within, I go ahead and knock, hoping I'll be able to think fast enough to come up with an excuse for whatever this is about.

"Come in," the director's deep voice calls, and I pop the door and step into a posh office with plush carpet, a leather couch, and a fancy wooden desk.

At least fifty years old with glasses and a receding hairline, Zee jumps up from his chair and hustles over, picking up a piece of paper from the desk on the way. Head tilted low, he looks observant, brilliant even, and I'm suddenly convinced there's no way I'll be able to pass this moment of truth.

Shaking, I make the snap judgment to give up now. If I beg, maybe he'll have mercy on me.

"Sir, I'm extremely sorry, but I have to tell you—"

He cracks a smile, showing some yellowed teeth as he extends the paper to me.

"I know all about it. Congratulations on a job well done!"

We lock eyes for a moment, and I notice him scanning me carefully. It feels like he's analyzing every inch of my face, not getting hung up on the bruise at all. But at the same time there's not the slightest sign of skepticism or concern.

It dawns on me that he fully sees me and has accepted that

it one glance, and gasp into my hand.

"Wait, what's this for?" I ask, at a complete loss to understand what's going on.

Ron Zee squints at me for a moment before breaking out into chuckles and then wagging a finger at me.

"Ah-ha, that's exactly the kind of discretion I was hoping for," he says, holding his hands behind his back as he stands up straight, beaming.

I take another gander at the slip of paper in my hand, trying to fathom why on earth he could be handing this out mere minutes into the workday following our disastrous girls' trip to the lake. I have a sneaking suspicion that everything I thought I knew is wrong.

It's a company bonus check made out to Alice Patterson for ten thousand dollars.

2

My hands feel clammy, and I keep forgetting to breathe. This is way more money than I've ever held at one time, as much as I'd make working here for over a quarter of a year, and they're throwing it at Alice *as a bonus*.

What would someone in HR do to get a bonus like this? They didn't sell anything, didn't pick stocks, didn't make investments. And the truth is I don't at all believe it's a mere coincidence that Alice is getting this after our weekend together at the lake.

It raises an important question. What did our company, Bedrock, get out of that weekend together that they feel like they need to pay ten grand for?

I try to be casual about giving Director Zee an appraising glance, but he seems satisfied, basking in my surprise and delight at the massive influx of cash.

The trouble though is I can't ask him the one question that's burning within my mind. What is this money for? What did Alice do to deserve this?

Because Alice would know what this is for, but if I ask too blatantly again I'll give away that I'm not her.

in the hopes of shaking some information out of him.

"Director Zee, I want to express my heartfelt gratitude for this. The confidence you and Bedrock have placed in me is deeply fulfilling. All I want to do is make a difference for this company and have it be appreciated," I say, gazing into his eyes like a lovestruck teenager.

His cheeks redden, and he scratches the back of his head.

"Yes, well, there are times when we're called upon to perform duties outside the norm, and not everybody is capable of that," he says. I'm hanging on every word, looking for clues, but he's giving me nothing.

I'm drawing a blank but can't leave until I know what Alice was really up to. This feels like my big chance to find out more about what was really happening this past weekend, and all the better if I get to pocket ten grand for it.

"Is there anything else that needs to be said?" I ask, hoping he'll take it from here.

He puts on a sly smirk and then backs up and returns to his desk, settling into his large black desk chair. He signals to the couch against the side wall, and I take a seat and glimpse a few things he's hiding behind the desk—a small wastebasket, a baseball bat, and a tennis racket.

Zee leans in my direction, one elbow on the desk, and pulls a bottle of whiskey out of a drawer.

"It's noon somewhere, right?" he says, proceeding to twist off the cap and drain a quarter of the bottle. Sucking through his teeth, he holds it out to me.

"No, thanks," I say, taken aback. If he wants to have a good buzz while at work, he probably managed it in one fell swoop. Setting the bottle back in the drawer, he gives me a sly smirk.

"My apologies. I should've recalled you ladies will be going

to be said. Have you ever come in here and really looked around?"

Eyes wide, I glance around the room, but he waves me off.

"I don't mean literally in here. I'm talking about all of Bedrock. There are over four hundred employees working here, and we've made this one of the premier financial firms in the country in five short years. When you look around, you'll see there are three kinds of people. Those who thrive, those who survive, and those who dive."

I nod blankly, wondering if I'm being mansplained to again. Maybe asking questions was a mistake and all I'm going to get is hot air. Surprisingly, he seems to notice my detachment.

"The reason I'm telling you this is that those who thrive in these challenging conditions make it into the big chairs, while others tread water or get chewed up and spit out. How many people here do you think could've done what you did?"

He stares at me, expecting an answer.

"Probably some," I say, and he raises his chin, squinting at me again.

"Not many, and look at what it cost you. You look like a train wreck."

Blinking, I realize what he's talking about and lightly touch the bruise on my face, feeling a slight sting. Am I to understand that he thinks I got this bruise doing whatever I was supposed to be doing for the company?

"It wasn't easy," I admit, and he nods in agreement.

"I'm sure it was brutal, but you got it done, and that's all that matters. And you've been rewarded for it. So here's what I want to know. We need people who can take on these kinds of extraordinary challenges. Can we count on you to do what the company needs to get ahead?"

gleam in Ron Zee's eyes, something conniving there that gives me pause. What was Alice doing for the company that demanded this kind of call for fealty?

But I'm here now, not Alice, and the only way I'm going to find answers is to keep diving deeper down the rabbit hole to see what kind of wonderland I've gotten into.

"Sir, serving Bedrock in whatever capacity it needs is my greatest honor," I say.

The director eyes the whiskey drawer again but leans back and puts his arms behind his head, his tie flopping askew against his side.

"So did you have a good weekend though?" he asks, and I can't tell if this is a continuation of the previous conversation or if he's now trying to make small talk.

I take a deep breath, wondering why he's asking, what he knows, and what he wants to get out of me.

"It didn't go the way I expected, let me tell you. Sometimes it makes no sense why people have to be so difficult," I say, getting caught up in a moment of reflecting and marveling at how in a few days instead of being at my desk working as a financial planner, I'm sitting here with a ten-thousand-dollar check and a different name.

Some light laughter escapes from Zee's mouth.

"If it weren't for that, we'd be out of a job," he says. "And what about the amigo from accounting. What's her name? I should know it."

"Taylor," I say before he grabs his computer mouse to start looking it up. Having her brought up seems like the perfect moment to rat her out for her fake résumé and seedy schemes with Wesley. "She has quite a wild side."

I'm hoping for a cue from Zee to go into the lies she told to get her job, maybe even implicate her in my death, but instead

something on his computer screen. It's Taylor's OnlyFans page, and I'm gobsmacked again. He knows about her modeling?

"Do you know what we call this?" he asks me with a straight face, a stray finger pointing at the screen, where thankfully the preview pictures are scandalous but not explicit.

I clear my throat, feeling awkward. "A side hustle?"

He shakes his head. "Leverage. Once you identify what someone needs, you can make them do what you want. That's what HR is all about," he says, swiveling his chair to take a long, appraising glance at Taylor, who's making a kissy face in the photo. "This one could prove surprisingly useful."

I nod glumly, watching my chance to get Taylor terminated slip away. So much for my revenge against the girl who planted a camera in the bathroom on me and came after me with a knife… twice. Oh well, with any luck she'll be arrested for murder and thrown in prison.

It's tempting to question how useful she'll be when behind bars for the rest of her life, but disagreeing with my boss doesn't seem like the right move.

"Yes, of course," I mutter.

I notice that the director appears to be focusing his attention much more on the computer screen, and it's making me uncomfortable. Right around when he starts mumbling to himself, I go ahead and get up and head for the door, bonus check in my pocket, hoping to find answers about Alice's special mission elsewhere.

But I hear him call out once I open the door, making me look back at the naughty grin on his face.

"Oh, Alice, one more thing. We've got a new hire on the fourth floor over in the financial services wing. Can you handle the usual company guidelines and regulations spiel?"

It's not a question, and I react instantly to the order.

fourth floor as well.

Shutting the door behind me, I search my recollection about any vacancies or new hires among the financial planners before I left, but I can't come up with anything, not so much as an empty desk.

When I've returned to my workstation, Janice isn't there, and I start looking around in various drawers and cabinets for paperwork relating to company rules and policies. It gets frustrating when I'm not able to find anything at all that'll help me know what to say. Shouldn't there be stacks of a company handbook around here for this very thing?

"Can I help you find something?" a voice asks, startling me as I'm on my tiptoes trying to reach onto a high shelf.

I glance over my shoulder and notice another one of the HR ladies, this one in her mid-thirties, if I'm not mistaken. It dawns on me that she was the one to give me the welcome speech on my first day. Shelley is her name, short curly black hair and a button nose.

"Yeah, I'm about to onboard a new hire but can't find the paperwork."

Without a moment's hesitation, she reaches behind a desk and produces a three-ring binder that she hands over to me. I take it and notice that all it has in it are a few blank sheets of white paper.

"But this is basically empty!" I say.

When I glance up at her, what I see stops me cold. Her guilty-pleasure look seems insatiable, and I have to bite my tongue to keep myself from gasping. There are no onboarding materials, no written rules and regulations, no employee handbook.

She'd made up everything she said to me. Wait a second,

socks? I'd been wearing them every day straight through to today because that was what she'd told me.

My embarrassment making my bruise itch, I take the empty binder and start my trek to the financial services floor. I have to come up with something to say fast and can scarcely remember any other nonsense Shelley pumped me full of a month ago in the blur of getting settled into work.

The elevator dings, letting me off on the fourth floor, and I feel my nerves start to flare as I walk around my old section of the office, one where people might have the best chance of recognizing me. Tilting my head so that my hair falls in front of my eyes, I shuffle through looking for anybody who might be new.

Glancing here and there, everybody seems the same, and for a second I wonder if Director Zee set this up as some kind of trick. Maybe there is no new employee. Despite his mischievous look, I conclude he was serious and keep going, almost making an entire loop around the floor.

There's only one corner of the office I have yet to look, and the realization comes with an uncomfortable feeling of dread.

I know where there's an empty desk on the fourth floor and start in that direction more slowly this time. There's no possible way there could be someone there already. I mean, I didn't quit and wasn't fired. Bedrock would have had no way of knowing I wouldn't be showing up for work this morning, no time to interview and hire someone on Labor Day.

But as I round the corner, sure enough I see that the desk I should be sitting at has a new occupant—a young man actually, early twenties in a dress shirt and tie. I catch a glimpse of mussy hair, bedhead not gel, and lightly tanned skin.

I stop right behind the cubicle, waiting a moment before

old chair. Between the check in my pocket and the person a few feet in front of me, an uncomfortable picture of what's going on starts to take shape.

I've been replaced before I even left.

3

It stings to realize that the place I'd staked my hopes on for a good life would do this to me, but I know this is only the tip of the iceberg. I take a sweeping look around the office to get a hold of myself.

I need to be chipper and welcoming, not mopey and whiny.

But I can't help but wonder if there's a single person here who's not completely corrupt. Who exactly wasn't expecting me to make it into work today, and does it have to do with the ten-thousand-dollar check in my pocket?

"Knock, knock," I say, rapping my knuckles against the corner of the cubicle, empty binder tucked under my arm and the biggest smile I can put on my face without suffering crippling agony from my bruise.

I step in as the guy turns around, his clean-shaven face with a gently sloping nose coming into view. Eyes the color of milk chocolate and a tuft to his hair from the bedhead.

For a moment we're both frozen in shock, me because of his magnetic appearance and him because of...you know.

"Ouch! What happened to you?" he asks with the voice of a punk band singer.

reveling in my replacement's inability to tell if I'm being serious or not. I savor telling the truth before it's on to more lies. "I'm Alice Patterson."

He flinches when we shake hands and I give him a firm grip. For some reason, I want him to know I mean business, which might come in handy when he inevitably turns out to be another cheating fraudster.

"I'm Miles Brewer. Nice to meet you."

I help myself to the chair next to his desk and put one leg over the other so that I can prop my important, empty binder up.

"Likewise. Welcome to Bedrock. I hope you're having a good first day. We've got a few things to discuss to help get you situated here, some policies and company rules, and then we'll be able to let you loose on our clients," I say, flipping the binder open to the first blank page.

"I'm ready," he says.

His gaze drifts to the binder, and I raise my leg a little to make the angle harder for him to see. He leans a little closer, and I raise the angle more until the binder is nearly parallel to my torso. Finally, he gives up trying to see what the paperwork says and refocuses his attention on me.

"I'm sure most of the terms of your employment were right on your contract," I say. "Remuneration, vacation days, sick leave, and of course grounds for dismissal, which include lateness, malfeasance in the workplace, substandard performance evaluations, violation of our social media policies, personal integrity concerns, and most importantly any errors or omissions with your application materials."

I appraise him carefully, expecting him to wince at any number of those, but he keeps his eyes on me with an easy half-smile. Not giving himself away right out of the gate is good, but I

me and Taylor with little trouble.

This desk could be fully vacant again by lunch. I tell myself it wouldn't be personal, but I have to admit to myself I wouldn't mind watching him walk away.

"OK," he says simply, eagerly even, which is the exact thing someone would say if they had lied to get their job and wanted to try to get away with it.

I close the binder and swallow, ready to move on from the ostensible reason for this visit and start digging deeper.

"Why don't you tell me about yourself?" I say, hoping he'll have at least rehearsed his made-up story.

"Why do you want to know about me?"

I jerk my head back a fraction of an inch.

"Because I'm in HR, you're new here, and we're going to be working together," I say with a curt nod for him to get on with it.

"We're going to be working together?"

I squint, trying to read into his calm face and relaxed demeanor, hands resting on his thighs. I'm supposed to be asking the questions, not him, and this is getting in the way of me extracting the answers I need.

"Not directly together, but we're in the same company, you know," I say, and he tips his head down as if I've disappointed him. For some reason, it makes me feel badly.

"Oh," he mutters.

"So please tell me about your background and how you got here," I say more firmly.

Miles gives me a wary look I have to deliberately straighten up to avoid withering against.

"Isn't that the whole point of résumés, so that you can quickly get everything you need to know about a person's background?"

turning away and putting my hand to my head.

"Yes, that's what a résumé is for, but perhaps there's something not on it you'd like to share. Do you have a problem with talking about yourself?"

When I'm looking away, I happen to see something on the desk, a wallet-size picture in a thin walnut frame. It's the only personal item I'd brought into work, a picture of the four of us in my immediate family before the car accident. Even with this bruise and the age difference, I'm worried this guy will recognize me from the picture.

"No, I don't mind talking about myself, but everything I'd say about myself is on the résumé anyway."

I scoff. Miles Brewer is one hundred percent hiding something.

"I don't have a copy of your résumé on me."

"That can be easily fixed," he says, leaning away to reach into his briefcase.

While he's doing that, I fake a cough and scoop up the photo from the desk, sliding it into my pocket right next to the bonus check I have for unknown reasons.

Miles hands me a piece of paper, this one with words printed on it. Aggravated either by his evasiveness or cuteness, I scan the page, where he has his education, work experience, and skills listed.

A part of me wants to laugh.

"There's not much here," I say, unable to keep myself from grinning. "You could've put down more."

"I only graduated in May. I haven't had time to do any more," he says. His straight face is making it impossible for me to take this seriously. No time to do any more. That is such a good one coming from a guy who made up everything here!

Clarkson University."

"That's correct."

"And am I supposed to believe this is a real school?"

When he narrows his eyes at me, I suppress a grin. He probably didn't expect to be called out so quickly. I like getting under his skin.

"Yeah, it's in Upstate New York, not far from the Canadian border."

I overexaggerate a nod.

"Making up a school far away doesn't mean we can't verify its existence. Are you trying to suggest you went there?"

"I'm not suggesting it," he says, and I nearly gasp until he snickers to himself at my reaction. "My diploma and transcript prove it."

"Sure. What kind of printer do you have?"

His cocky look fades, and confusion returns.

"What do you mean?" He's getting antsy in his chair. It's only a matter of time until he cracks. Then I'll be able to get anything I want out of him.

"I mean, what printer did you use to print the diploma and transcript?"

For a moment, he's speechless, his mouth hanging open, and I'm oddly finding myself loving every second of it. Is this what working in HR is like every day, flabbergasting cute guys? I could get used to this.

"Let me ask you one question. What would make you think that I've printed a fake diploma, claimed to go to a college I didn't go to, or that I made up an entire school to put on my résumé?"

We lock eyes for a moment before I break into a furtive grin.

"I'm not the one who wrote this résumé, and it's not my job

I say.

He's shaking his head like it would rotate fully around his neck if it could. He's growing flustered, and it's adding some color to his cheeks.

"Well, it is."

"That's not an argument."

"Yes, it is," he shoots back.

"Name three of the dorms."

"Moore, Hamlin, and Powers."

I sigh. "One of those sounds made up, but alright. Name two professors you had."

"Really? Ugh. Alan Bowman and John DeJoy."

I glare at him. "It took you a long time to answer that."

Miles nearly jumps out of his chair.

"No, it didn't. They're economics and finance professors. That's what I majored in!"

I watch him calmly but skeptically. He did answer fast enough to at least suggest he did a minimal amount of research to back up his lies. But I don't have all day and need to move on to more important company issues, namely why I was being replaced before anyone should've known I wouldn't be coming into work.

"When did you hear about the open financial planner position here?" I ask.

Miles takes a deep breath and eyes me warily. He seems unsettled, but if I didn't know any better I'd say he likes it. Or am I imagining things?

"The beginning of last week."

"And you replied right away?"

"Yeah, I'd already moved here and was looking for work in the area."

"When was your interview?"

I nod, putting the timeline together in my head. Someone had been planning for me to be gone from the very beginning of last week. This wasn't a surprise reaction to the disaster of Hochatown between me, Alice, and Taylor. No, someone was planning this outcome and was interviewing my replacement while I was sitting in Miles's chair busily not doing a job I didn't know how to do.

I wonder if it's possible someone figured out that math, ahem, is not my strong suit, but I quickly reject that idea. I hadn't even had one performance evaluation yet, and there had been no criticism. So why plan to get rid of me?

"When were you offered the job?" I ask. When he takes a moment to think, my gut reaction is to assume he's going to make something up, but a small part of me wants to believe he's actually trying to remember correctly.

He rubs his chin, and I watch his skin pull along his jawline.

"It was later in the day Wednesday. Seems they could've just offered it to me at the interview, but I guess they needed a little more time."

I nod absently, recalling that Wednesday was the same day that Alice, Taylor, and I had decided we'd be taking a trip together that weekend. Apparently those plans made somebody here comfortable enough to offer someone else my job.

A growing feeling of agitation blooms in my chest as I start to see where this is going and what it means for me.

"Do you recall who conducted your interview?" I ask, and his strange look immediately returns. He's skeptical of something, and I don't know what it is.

Miles's mouth cracks open, and I start to get the impression he's afraid to say it. All I can do is watch him carefully and spit it out, because that name is my first step to finding out who is behind this.

I freeze, my mind reeling as I quickly put together why he's been giving me these strange looks and acting awkwardly while I introduced myself and asked some of these questions. He must think I'm completely insane, having interviewed him myself and then questioning him about it like I have no memory of it, which of course I don't.

Laughing must only make me seem crazier, but I have to do something to get through this, because I'm not done with him yet.

"I'm so sorry about that. Since having this terrible accident, my head hasn't been screwed on straight," I say, gesturing to the impact crater on my face. "Can I ask you one more question to help me get my bearings?"

He eyes me blankly, like he doesn't know what he's witnessing, and I take that as enough of a sign to continue.

"In the interview we had together, do you remember me saying anything about the person you were replacing, Emily Marks?"

Miles appears reluctant, skittish even, and I'm not surprised considering what I've been putting him through. Usually I'm not the crazy one. He taps his fingernail against the desk in a way that makes me impatient. Finally, he shrugs.

"Not really. All you said was that there was a sudden vacancy you needed to fill quickly," he says.

I glance at him, hoping he'll go on and give me something better. That wasn't the answer I was looking for.

"OK, I lied about that being the last question. Did I say anything about why Emily Marks wouldn't be coming back?"

Miles brightens up as a lightbulb goes off in his head, and for a moment I imagine staying blissfully ignorant a little longer so that I can keep admiring his smile, but I have to find out what happened to me.

ugly phrase never sounding so sweet.

Suddenly it all makes sense. What happened at the cabin, the check in my pocket, the smart boy with the chocolate eyes next to me.

Alice had been asked to get rid of me, which means someone at Bedrock wants me dead.

4

"Are you alright? Hello?"

I'm in a daze, my heart pounding, as far from alright as humanly possible. I keep trying to piece together what happened, but I'm getting stuck on the simplest question: Why?

Why would someone at a huge national financial firm want me dead? I was nothing more than a floundering new hire who'd been here for a few weeks. Told off, fired, and thrown out? Sure. But dead? Come on!

A glance at Miles tells me he's borderline freaking out now that I appear catatonic, and I realize I have to get out of here.

"That concludes our meeting. Thank you very much for speaking with me. Now if you don't mind, I really must be going," I say like a robot, getting to my feet so fast that I actually stumble.

Miles hops out of his chair like lightning and steadies me, or maybe everything seems to be happening so fast only because my mind is churning a mile a minute.

I try to smile at him politely and then shift away. His lies hadn't come out during the meeting, but I'm sure they're there nonetheless. Whatever he has going on pales in comparison to

into now.

If Alice was sent to Hochatown for some kind of hit job on me, there's no better place for me to try to find out what's happening than right in her shoes.

"I'll let you know if I have any questions," Miles says regretfully, watching me go.

"Uh-huh, great," I say, starting away from the cubicle right into the path of an old lady with cotton for hair and a pearl necklace. "Excuse me."

"Looks like my first meeting is here anyway," Miles says, approaching.

It dawns on me that he's already gotten a meeting with a client, something I hadn't done once in my three weeks on the job. No doubt this old lady needs help with her retirement and the management of her finances.

Miles would be the perfect guy to help with that...and a lot of other things.

Stalking away with my head down, dark-blonde hair over my face, binder tucked under my arm, and fists clenched at my side, I chide myself for the thought. The last thing I need is any kind of entanglement with another serial liar like Wesley, especially not when I've finally found out what was going on during our girls' trip.

Motoring to the elevators, I think back to when I was sitting with Alice and Taylor in the screened porch during the rainstorm. I'd asked them point-blank what they were up to. No wonder Alice didn't answer truthfully!

Nothing makes a conversation more awkward than letting something slip like, "I've been sent here to kill you."

I push the button and wait for the doors to open, glad no one else is around to distract me from my stampeding thoughts. *Ding*, the doors open, and I step in.

bizarre offer to take control of my life and claim that I could continue working here. It wasn't until I flatly turned her down that she attacked me along with Taylor, who was ready to cut me to pieces.

I conclude that Alice was somehow going to circumvent her order to kill me, which became her plan B. Having me as her possession was her preference, and I have to assume she'd try to get me to hide or lie low, perhaps even fake my own death, so that she could still get the ten thousand dollars.

It's hard to believe it wasn't even forty-eight hours ago that all of this took place.

The elevator doors open, and I hustle back to the human resources department, ducking in without looking anyone in the eye. Janice is at her desk again, as is Shelley. The men in the office see my body but not me, and I hope they don't become suspicious that I'm not Alice.

I thought I wore loose clothes, but maybe these aren't loose enough.

Plopping down at my seat and waking the computer, I stretch my fingers as I prepare to get down to work. No, definitely nothing to do with HR or whatever Alice would normally be doing right now. Forget that.

It's time to dig in to try to find answers about who planned for my replacement, who gave the order to send Alice after me, and why I needed to be terminated both professionally and personally.

The natural first suspect is Human Resources Director Ron Zee, who admittedly gave the order to Alice and followed through with the check for ten thousand dollars. But he's someone I'd never met and had never even heard of, and I can't imagine him having a vendetta against me.

I'm doubtful he's behind the whole thing, but he must know

only worth ten thousand dollars? Seems awfully cheap to me, but I might be biased.

Letting my thoughts and speculations run wild won't give me any concrete confirmations, but setting my fingers loose on this keyboard will. I bring up the HR Slack channel and start looking around for any private messages, especially from Ron Zee. Although there's plenty of communication, I can't find anything from him referencing me or any kind of special assignment.

But what I do find quickly becomes mesmerizingly disturbing. The channel for financial planners was nothing but boring drivel, but the folks in this department seem to have a particularly aggressive interpretation of what it means to be managing the people around the office.

There are extensive message threads, at least a hundred, exploring bits of office gossip, tracking office romances, and commenting on people's appearances, clothing styles, and personal habits. There's a bet going about when a lady in the compliance department will have a nervous breakdown. The HR agents seem to enjoy pitting employees against each other to create bitter rivalries until someone quits or acts out enough to get fired.

It's hard to keep my mouth closed as I look through all of the mean-spirited, manipulative things everyone here is doing around the office. If the other financial planners knew about this, there'd be a riot.

But there's very little from Ron Zee except for blanket announcements, none of which are salacious or pertinent to my search. Alice wasn't very active either, although she didn't hold back from sharing her snide, prudish opinions on occasion.

When I scroll a little more, I hit something that stands out. A thread is titled, "What's Wrong with the New Girl?" Posted two

accurate. It's about me, and I know this isn't going to be pretty.

Yes, Shelley had quickly chimed in laughing about how I wore black socks every day, but otherwise the comments are pretty petty and simplistic. They call me clueless, pathetic, hired for my looks. They suggest that the retail finance department managers only brought me in to get into my pants. A half-dozen comments argued over how I should work out more or dress differently.

The very last comment is from early last week, and weirdly it's from someone listed only as "Unnamed User." I didn't know anyone could get on the company Slack channels without having their real name listed. There's no picture, and it's not a reply to anything else. All it has are a few words I find highly inflammatory.

"She never should've set foot in here."

I look at that and grit my teeth, easily making the mental jump to the attempt on my life. Considering this was posted right around when the listing for my job went public for Miles to find, I have a strong sense that this person is involved in getting Alice to try to kill me.

My hackles raised, I glare at that message on the screen. Guess what. I'm still here, and Alice is the one in a body bag, so I'll set foot wherever I like. I make myself a promise. *I'm going to find out who you are and make you pay for what you did to me.*

Although there are people around me in the office, I feel so alone. My dream of having a good job and a decent life here was always a fantasy. Everyone is crooked, HR appears to be conducting weird social experiments on people, and I can't simply get by and learn a real job without someone deciding I need to be snuffed out of existence.

When the Slack channel proves both too useless and infuriating, I switch to Alice's phone, which I start going through with

happening to me.

Gone are the vague worries about somebody contacting Alice out of the blue and getting concerned if I don't answer the phone right way. Alice's aloof and pretentious nature alienated most people anyway. But now I'm trying to dig through her email and messages for anything about what she was really planning to do to me at the lake.

There's not much here other than some receipts for music she purchased and downloaded. As I saw on Taylor's phone, there are no texts between Taylor and Alice here either. Nothing from Ron Zee. It's beginning to become clear that whatever conversations that took place to arrange this weren't done online where they could be recorded and dredged up later.

Everything that took place to set me up occurred face to face, and that's the same way I'm going to have to get to the bottom of this. The thought crosses my mind to get up and march right back to Director Zee to demand an explanation, but that's the exact moment when the door to the office swings open, and he steps through.

He's breathing heavily, his eyes looking like they'll pop out of his head, and everyone drops what they're doing to turn to him.

"Sorry to interrupt, but we have an emergency situation. I need everyone in the department to meet in the conference room. Right now!"

Pursing his lips from the doorway, Director Zee glances at me out of the corner of his eye, saying tons more with a look than with his urgent announcement.

Now I get to be at the center of a companywide emergency. Great.

5

Finding the conference room is easy, since I can follow everyone else, but sorting through my conflicting emotions is much more difficult.

Somehow what is happening to me seems to be spilling out into the open, and all I can do is stand here and wait to hear about what exactly that entails. The entire HR staff, roughly about twenty-five of us, jam into a conference room featuring an oval-shaped table and a bank of windows looking out at downtown Dallas.

I don't make it in quickly enough to grab one of the seats, which leaves me standing against the back wall between Janice and Shelley, who I think keeps looking at me strangely, but I can't be sure. The last thing I need is somebody figuring out I'm not who I say I am, especially in the midst of an emergency.

Director Zee steps in last and closes the door behind himself, remaining there as if to block anyone from exiting before he's finished. Watching everyone carefully, he runs a hand through his thinning hair, and I feel my nerves suddenly flare up.

tors has arrived at the building claiming that they want to turn us inside out. We don't know exactly what they're looking for, but it's our job to make sure they don't have any problems, if you know what I mean. So let's steer them in the right direction, give them the right version of anything they're asking for, and try to get them out of here as quickly as possible," he explains.

Someone in one of the chairs raises a hand, and Zee takes off his glasses to wipe his brow in annoyance.

"Can you tell us who the investigators are with?" asks an older man who is wringing his hands nervously.

Zee glares at him for a moment, appearing reluctant to answer, but he eventually caves under the scrutiny of twenty-five sets of eyes.

"I haven't seen them with my own eyes, but the report is that they're with the FBI," he says, causing a stir of murmuring around the room.

I can relate. It should've been obvious to me that the McCurtain County Sheriff's Office wouldn't chase me all the way to Dallas, but the unknowns loom large in my mind and start to burn on my tongue, but I definitely can't talk about this in front of everyone.

Is the FBI here investigating my death? Did Taylor or someone tip them off that my murder had been orchestrated from within the Bedrock organization? What throws me off the most is not having a clue what the FBI is really here for. Either we have the same mission to find out who is really behind my death, or they're here to find me and take me away for what I did to Alice.

All I know is I have to talk to Director Zee immediately to find out what he knows. I never imagined I'd need Emily to come back so soon, but with a little information I can twist, I

on to those who want me dead.

"What does CEO Roberts think of this?" another man asks, getting an aggressive response from Zee, who extends a hand, palm out.

"That's the last time anyone should say her name today. She has no knowledge of what this is about and has no position on how these matters are being handled other than being in favor of our cooperation notwithstanding the best interests of the company. Now, that's enough. Go out there and brush them off. Anyone who makes a mistake today or causes trouble is going to find themselves without a job."

That inspiring declaration gets everyone to their feet, and Director Zee cracks the door open and allows the HR staff to leave. When I start to get close, he locks eyes with me for a moment and then slips out through the door before I can get to him.

Grumbling to myself, I imagine I'm going to have to chase him down the hall or stalk him back to his office, but as soon as I leave the room I feel a hand close around my arm, pulling me in the opposite direction from where everyone else is going.

It's Director Zee, who clearly has it in mind to have a conversation as much as I do, but his increasingly surly demeanor, so at odds with how he was earlier, makes me dread it. When we round the corner into a secluded section of the hall, I can't hold my tongue any longer.

"I think it's time you tell me where the idea to get rid of Emily Marks really came from."

Before I'm done talking, Director Zee has wheeled around on me, pushing me against the wall so that my back smacks against it, and he looms over me from inches away.

"What happened to that great sense of discretion I praised

between this company and Emily's death," he says, glaring at me, and I'm shocked at the feeling like he might hit me if I don't say the right thing.

Too bad for him I've always been too stupid to be intimidated.

"No relationship between the company and her death? Really? You don't think they're going to figure it out? This is the FBI. Even if I don't say a word to them, even if they never get their hands on this..."

I'm reaching into my pocket to pull out the ten-thousand-dollar check he'd given me earlier, but for some reason all I can feel is the picture of my family that I'd gotten from my old desk when I went to see Miles Brewer. What happened to my ten thousand dollars?

Ron Zee instantly notices my stricken look and cracks a smirk.

"That's exactly right. You're not going to tell or show them anything. These conversations never happened. And if they do manage to find you, I expect you to live up to your word."

I squint, tired of looking at his yellow teeth and smelling his boozy breath. He clearly didn't stop with that bottle of whiskey in his desk after I'd left.

"My word about what? What are you saying?"

He leers closer, and now we're standing toe to toe.

"What you said about rising to the occasion for the company if there should ever be such a need. Lo and behold, we may be in such a situation now, and I expect you to do the right thing."

Blinking and squirming, I try to edge away from him, but he's not letting me go anywhere. But even more uncomfortable from his close presence is what he's suggesting.

"You expect me to take full responsibility for Emily's death?"

discussion about me dying when I'm standing right here. I wonder if Alice has it easier and is laughing from wherever she is in the afterlife.

"If that's what the company needs you to do in order to make this problem go away, you'll do it, right?"

I feel like Director Zee hasn't blinked in a full minute, his unwavering eyes fixed on me and his glasses magnifying them.

"You don't think there's a limit to that? What good would it do me to help the company if I have to spend the rest of my life in prison? Didn't anyone think through what would happen if the authorities got involved?" I say, my facade cracking.

There are so many ways this could go badly for me, but Zee doesn't seem to care about any of them.

"It was your job to do this right, and you'd better finish it."

My gut feeling is to ask why, but I can hear the threat in his voice loud and clear. That gleam in his eye says it all, that if I don't take the fall then I could end up dead for real. It's starting to dawn on me that becoming Alice hasn't put me in the clear as neatly as I'd like.

And the last thing I want to do is make waves when this corporate four-eyes is raging as hard as the one-eyed guy at the lake.

"So what do you want me to do? I assume I shouldn't be going with the others to try to mediate with the FBI."

Zee mercifully backs off a little, the temperature seeming to drop now that I'm playing along more with what he wants. I'm grateful to have him no longer right in my face, but we hear footsteps and have to stand awkwardly in the hall together anyway until our coworker passes out of earshot.

This time, Zee leans closer in a less aggressive manner, whispering instead of sneering.

long lunch. Try not to draw any attention to yourself."

More footsteps echo from down the hall, and immediately Zee starts off in the opposite direction, as if we were never talking to begin with. I'm left there up against the wall feeling exposed in all kinds of ways, and it's not a good sign when my best option is to run and hide for a while.

I'm sure the FBI has never had to contend with that kind of brilliant strategy. The bruise on my face is going to be like a beacon for them anyway. How am I supposed to sneak out of here when they could be everywhere?

I smile faintly at the pair of men walking side by side around the hall corner, one brushing my front as he passes and snickers about it to his companion.

I glare at them from behind. My new identity has much less value than it did, the check I had is somehow gone, and the faith I have in this company is at rock bottom.

Trudging back in the direction of my desk, I wonder how this could possibly get any worse, and I'm starting to wonder if I'll even still be working here tomorrow. Another death threat might be the only way they can get me to come back here, but I'm still reluctant about it even though the alternative seems to be federal prison.

The HR office is abuzz now with people moving briskly in and out, and I have to limp out of the way of Shelley, who appears ready to bowl right over me. Janice is typing furiously at her desk, and I go ahead and take a seat next to her, trying to get my head straight about how I'm going to get out of here and where I'm going to go for the next couple of hours.

Shutting down the computer seems like the best thing to do, making it seem like I haven't been here in case the FBI comes in, but when I reflexively reach over for the mouse, I feel something is off and look over.

stuck on the mouse, and I pull it away feeling like this is a little weird. That feeling intensifies times one thousand when I see what's been written on the note.

"Hi, Emily."

6

My fingers tingle holding this tiny slip of paper, which with only a few scribbles on it has torn apart everything I thought was going on.

Someone knows.

I jerk to look around the office so hard it makes my neck hurt, but I don't see anyone conspicuously walking away or glancing in my direction to acknowledge noticing that I've received this wretched note.

It's difficult to sort out what this means. The FBI is in the building investigating my death, and yet somebody here has figured out that I'm not Alice Patterson, who I thought I was doing a fine job of pretending to be.

Breathing rapidly, I try to think back to recall any particularly suspicious looks that might've signaled recognition, but I can't come up with anything. Considering I was in the hall with Director Zee, that leaves everybody else in the universe as a possible culprit for this.

Janice is still pounding on the keyboard next to me, so into it that her dark-brown hair flowing back onto her shoulders bounces a bit when she smacks the space bar. I don't know her

find a different way to tell me than this.

"Do you know who left this on my desk?" I ask, holding up the orange square.

Blinking as if from a trance, Janice turns to me and focuses on what I'm holding.

"No, not a clue. What does that say?"

"Nothing!" I nearly shout as she leans closer. Clenching my fist, I crush the little paper before she can get a good look at it.

I need to calm down and think things through before I do anything stupid to make my life worse than it already is. It's not like the FBI would sneak in here and plant a sticky note with my real name on it if they knew what I was doing.

But it's easy enough to imagine how any odd person around the office who figured this out could make my life a nightmare. What would I do to avoid someone telling federal agents that I was involved in the death of a girl in the office whom I then went on to impersonate? Probably right around anything.

I figure Janice would go right back to typing, but instead she continues looking at me curiously, which makes me nervous. Did she actually see what was written on the note? My nerves keep making everything fuzzy, and I remind myself that I'm supposed to be getting out of here.

Janice takes another dejected look at her computer screen, leans hard against her seat back, and sighs.

"This is such a pain. I can't believe of all days we have to fend off an investigation today," she says, and I almost pity her for the minor nuisance she's experiencing compared to the potentially life-altering implications for me. "We're going out after work, right?"

Although she has her fingers draped over her eyes and face, she doesn't need to see to know that Shelley is cruising by in boots that thump against the floor with every step.

The conversation is a welcome distraction from my macabre thoughts of an imminent perp walk out of the building.

"But it's only Tuesday," I say.

Janice looks at me between her fingers as if she can't believe I really said that.

"Are you saying you aren't going to need a drink after this?" she asks with a raised eyebrow.

I swallow and nod. Game, set, and match on that argument.

"I don't know how anybody around here can go more than two days of work without wanting to get drunk as a skunk," Shelley says, stopping at her desk a short ways behind us.

I don't bother pointing out that nobody had to work Monday.

Janice chuckles along with Shelley.

"Alright then, sounds like a girls' night! I'll let the others know."

I tilt my head to be able to see Shelley's broad smile, which proves infectious. Who knows, maybe if I can make it to the end of the day without being behind bars I'll want to join them.

"Not the one in the compliance department though," Shelley says firmly. "She's crazy, and I could use that money."

The work managing the FBI investigation suddenly takes a back seat to office gossip for the two of them, a live reenactment of the Slack channel, and I use the opportunity to slip away for my extended lunch, which may involve some drinking too if this stress headache persists.

I smile as much as I can to the ladies without hurting myself, jam the crumpled note in my pocket where my ten-thousand-dollar check should be, and march out of the HR office into the greater sixth-floor office space, where the bank of elevators waits in the distance.

The cubicles all run to about chest height, and I do my best without ridiculously scuttling along the floor like a crab.

Out of the corner of my eye, I notice a group huddled off to the right around an employee in his cubicle. The bright-yellow FBI jackets are circling around a man whose face is beet red, his arms waving wildly. I can hear him shouting but can't make out specifically what's being said.

All of a sudden, one of the agents turns his head in my direction, and I crouch a little lower and double-time it to the elevators, keeping my eyes fixed ahead of me. I have to get out of here, and I realize I'm holding my breath and listening for someone to call after me or chase me down.

I'm shuffling along as fast as I can, hoping I don't collide with anyone as I cross this cavernous space. As if having the floor crawling with FBI agents isn't enough, it's possible the person who gave me this note with my real name on it could call after me as well. That would be quite a can of worms.

The last cubicle passes away, and I've moved far enough along that I'm not in easy eyeshot of the agents haranguing that Bedrock employee. I start to think I'm in the clear and straighten up in front of the elevator doors when the loud chime of the elevator rings, signaling that one has arrived at this floor and is about to open.

Caught off guard, I have a half a second to dive out of the way to avoid whoever is arriving at this floor, presumably another cadre of murder-investigating Feds on the hunt for a woman in her early twenties with dirty-blonde hair and a facial bruise that looks like a bowling ball.

The doors slide open ominously, and I'm still standing there like a deer in headlights when I realize it's mostly empty and doesn't contain anybody wearing a sleek navy windbreaker with bright-yellow lettering. But my eyes widen, and I gasp anyway.

the elevator with a big smile and something in his hand.

After he practically shouted my alias, I'm on high alert in case any of the agents heard it. It looks like he's about to keep talking, and I rush forward, putting my hand over his mouth and pushing him back into the elevator.

He bumps against the back wall, and I try to reach across the car to push the bottom button for the first floor while covering his mouth at the same time. It doesn't exactly work, as I can tell when his loud voice echoes in my ears again.

"What is going on?" he says, panicked, a flush adding a little more color to his lightly tanned skin. His brown eyes are wide and starting to become bloodshot.

"Shh," I say, reaching over again to push the button to the ground floor. The doors can't close fast enough, but eventually we find ourselves alone in the secluded space. "What are you doing here?"

He flinches, coming back to his senses, and raises his hand again. He's got my check in his hand and is giving it back to me.

"I noticed you dropped this after you left our meeting," he says, watching me with a warm look.

I'm not sure what has me more surprised, seeing that check again or having Miles hand it to me when there are a dozen places within a mile where he could've forged Alice's signature and gotten it cashed.

This might be the most incredible thing anyone has ever done for me. What kind of trick is he pulling?

7

I take the check and slip it back into my pocket, promising myself to be more careful this time. Either it's evidence that the company is involved in my death or a big chunk of money I could really use.

Miles is standing comfortably next to me, and we do the thing where we try to look at anything but each other. A curiosity creeps into my mind about what he thinks about me, but I have to remind myself this isn't really who I am.

These clothes, this hair, this face, this name, it's all fake, and I'm sure he doesn't deserve to see the real me anyway. I haven't found out how he's a big liar like the rest of us yet, but it's only a matter of time until he slips up.

That doesn't mean we can't have a little fun in the meantime.

"We went by my floor," he says as the elevator continues to descend.

"I know."

He swallows, and his relaxed pose goes rigid.

"I should really be getting back to my desk."

I cast a sidelong glance at him when I say, "We're going on a lunch date."

good chance I'm about to serve twenty to life. He sneaks a look in my direction, seeming to grow paler, and I imagine it's because he's intimidated by my beauty...or injuries.

"It's not lunch hour yet."

I scoff and cross my arms over my stomach, wondering how difficult and awkward he's going to be about it. Maybe this was a mistake.

"If there's one day when nobody is going to notice if you take lunch a few minutes early, it's today."

The elevator continues to descend, and I wait for him to offer another protest, reach out to hit a button on the elevator to go back to his floor, or do anything to make a fuss one more time to push me to the breaking point and convince me to go on alone.

The doors slide open, and we step out together side by side without looking back.

Good choice.

He's standing straighter now. And I notice he walks with poise, confident. This is already more like it, and I'm glad the matter is settled. If only everything else could be as easy as picking up a guy in an elevator.

The building's ground floor is an open atrium. While there are plenty of people around, I'm not seeing any more FBI agents. I don't delude myself that I'm in the clear and want to get somewhere more concealed fast, but simply being out of the office makes me think some distance and a break could help me figure things out.

We naturally turn to the adjoining food court, which is a short ways away in the connected next building over. A lot of business people are around in suits from various companies, and we blend in easily, another young woman and man simply climbing the corporate ladder and definitely not trying to escape a murder rap while impersonating the deceased.

my side, like we've been working on an intense project one-on-one and are taking a break before breathless exhaustion sets in.

After a tip of my head, we veer toward a counter serving arepas, meat sizzling on the grill and an overweight man in a greasy white apron waving a spatula like a ninja.

"We'll take two," Miles says, stepping up at exactly the right time, but I reach for my purse.

"I've got it," I say, since it was my idea, but Miles waves me off, a card in his hand.

"Don't worry about it," he says as if he couldn't care less about the money.

"Alright," I say, more gratified than I should be. It's probably for the best since the FBI may be monitoring my transactions for all I know. Will I ever be able to live a normal life again?

But I return to my senses and remember this is probably some kind of scam to sucker me in and make me reveal something he can exploit for his personal gain. I'm not that soft to bite on another hook over an arepa, and as we carry our plates, I vow to find out what he's really up to once and for all.

We park at a table close to the middle but a fair ways away from the door leading into the Bedrock offices, giving me time to get up and bolt if the FBI starts storming the place. Miles takes a seat next to me, his tie twisted in front of his light-blue dress shirt.

I get the sense that he's slim and doesn't really work out, but he's carefree and composed in a way that feels like a relief after so many tense conversations about who killed whom and who's going to be held responsible for it. Plus, he chews with his mouth closed.

"This lunch date can't be going very well if you keep eyeing the exit like that," he says with a half-smile. "You expecting company?"

"No, no one is going to bother us."

"What if I'm supposed to be meeting with someone?" he asks suggestively.

I narrow my eyes.

"You don't have a girlfriend. You just moved here from no man's land in central Maine."

"Upstate New York."

"Same difference."

He glances at me for a moment, and I can see I'm getting a rise out of him.

"What about you? How'd you end up working for Bedrock, Alice?"

I blink, almost having forgotten that I'm not myself until he used Alice's name. It feels like it's polluted the moment, like this simple thing of having lunch with someone is happening to someone else and not me because it's not my name coming out of his mouth. A part of me wants to gush the whole truth and shout, "I'm Emily!"

But one person out there already knows who I am, and that's already too many.

"Nothing too complicated. I studied hard in school, tried to do everything right, and now I'm working here," I say, as Alice might.

Miles peers at me, setting his half-eaten arepa down.

"You don't sound exactly thrilled about it."

I look away back to the entrance, wondering if I'm losing control of myself by saying this.

"I think it's been demystifying for me working here. In school everything is black and white, good and bad, but here you can really see how everyone has something to hide."

He chuckles, covering his lips with a finger as he eyes me.

couldn't possibly believe it.

"You have no idea."

"Sure, I bet you do. What, do you cheat at Wordle, only tip nineteen percent, wear the same black socks two days in a row?"

He's looking at me like he really wants to know, like I'm the only other person in this crowded food court, and I see my chance.

"I'll tell you something as soon as you tell me how you doctored your résumé," I say, raising an eyebrow. "You don't have to pretend any longer. I know there's something."

He purses his lips, and now he's glancing around like the FBI might be bursting in on him. His dark-brown eyes wash over me again, like he's seeing me and figuring something out. It's exciting and terrifying.

"Sheesh, you're a ball buster, but I'll tell you," he says, and I'm sitting on my hands to keep from pumping my fists. I knew it! "Everything on there is right, but I did leave something off. I have more experience than I let on. Truth be told, it may not be good experience."

I stare at his strange mixture of regret and pride. It takes a nod for me to get him to keep going before I have to wrangle it out of him.

"Early this year, I had an internship with H&R Block helping people with tax returns and such, but because of the finance program I was in, I also was assisting with the management and got a look at some of the business financials. It turns out they were charging people some unnecessary fees, so I alerted the authorities, who took action and got people their money back."

I gaze at him quizzically. My mind is having a meltdown, not able to compute any of that.

"You're a...a whistleblower?" I say, the word so strange on my tongue that I'm barely able to get it out.

"Guilty as charged. I think you can understand how some companies may not be interested in hiring someone who might keep an eye out to help customers."

He's talking about his employability, but I'm still stuck on when a company was scamming customers, he exposed them and made them do the right thing even when he could've turned a blind eye.

That's so...so... What's the word for that? It reminds me of when he gave me my check back a short while ago.

"I can't even believe you would do these things. It's probably cost you a lot of money."

He shakes his head like he doesn't care, and I realize he doesn't. He comes from a comfortable background and went to college. His approach to money and life is like night and day compared with mine.

And yet he's right here with me working for this same company doing these terrible things. He's like a lamb that wandered into the wolf's den. It starts to burn me up.

He smirks and leans forward. "OK, now it's your turn. What's your dark secret?"

I laugh-cry as he puts the spotlight on me and start shaking my head.

"I can't do that now. Your bad thing is so good. I can't give you some real dirt on me."

Miles's look softens, and if this table weren't between us, I'd probably steal a hug from him.

"Come on. It can't be that bad. You can tell me."

I'm thrown for a loop and getting unreasonably emotional. Why are my eyes welling up all of a sudden? This strange feeling comes over me, and I realize it's because I'm embarrassed by myself.

lutely everything you know about me is false."

He winces in confusion, which feels like a stake to my heart.

"That can't possibly be true. Tell me, and it'll be alright. I'll keep it to myself, promise."

I cross my arms over my stomach and feel my bruise starting to ache from the pressure I'm feeling.

"You probably would, wouldn't you? But don't you see? That's exactly the problem. That thing you are—I keep forgetting the word for it—I can never be like that. I've never been able to afford not to lie."

His calm look at me is like a ray of light, but I don't want his sympathy.

"Telling the truth is free, Alice," he says, but I have a ten-thousand-dollar check in my pocket that begs to differ.

I'm backed into a corner, and something in my head feels like it's breaking. If the truth is free, how come it feels like it'll cost so much?

My lips pinch, and my jaw is quivering. I cast my eyes around again at the crowd, looking for help, but there's no escape from this prison I've created for myself. I've had enough, and something snaps. I cast him a cold, hard look, in disbelief that he's beaten me down to this point.

"You want to know the truth? I'll tell you the truth. This company you're working for, Bedrock, is more corrupt, unethical, and dangerous than anything you've ever encountered or could possibly imagine. And if you stick around, it'll corrupt you too. So here's what you should do. Run! Leave this place right this second and keep living your sweet, beautiful life somewhere else before you get dragged into something you can't escape from."

Miles's face slackens, and he stares at me blankly. I worry I've scared him with my outburst, and his stunned look continues

to spit out something about if he has anything to say, but instead I glance around the food court again.

That's when I see something out of the corner of my eye. A shape, a body, a person there watching me one second who disappears into the crowd when I try to focus in on him.

Someone's been watching me.

8

M iles sputters back to life, but he's giving me a skeptical look with a sly grin. Figures the one time I try to tell the truth I'm not taken seriously.

"But Bedrock is an amazing place to work," he insists. "What Candace Roberts has done building this company from scratch is breathtaking and has created so much wealth for so many people."

I nod distantly, incapable of even giving him a tenth of my attention any longer. There's someone here who doesn't belong, and I anxiously scan the crowd for a glimpse of my mystery stalker. My gut reaction is that the guy from the lake has returned, and he's lurking outside of my field of view like he did at the cabin.

There wasn't time to notice anything distinct about his features, not his hair color or even whether he had one eye. All I sensed was someone staring at me before he moved. I caught a glimpse of black clothing, but not a suit like everyone else. More like a black windbreaker.

Not one of the FBI, not anyone running any kind of an investigation, this is someone who is coming after me.

continues, so wrapped up in his happy spiel about Bedrock that he hasn't noticed I'm on another planet. "The Q Fund in particular has had double-digit returns like clockwork since the company was founded. It's a stroke of genius. The others are good too, but that's the crown jewel."

"The Q Fund, yes," I say absently, vaguely recalling hearing about that during my first days. That was the one we were supposed to steer all of our clients to, the sure moneymaker for them and for us.

I start to wonder how the guy from the bar who nearly strangled me to death on the beach could've followed me here. Wouldn't he be previously hurt? Maybe it's not even him. What if it's the person who put the note saying "Hi, Emily" on my mouse? That handwriting didn't seem distinctly masculine or feminine, neither neat nor messy. It could've been anyone.

That same feeling I had so often at the lake hits me again. I'm being hunted, someone is messing with me, and the last thing I want to do is stray from the pack so I can be picked off. I glance around again, having the vaguest sense that someone is around and watching me, but I can't be sure.

"Hello, Earth to Alice," Miles says, waving, and I give him the best faint smile I can muster under the circumstances. "I'm sorry if all that financial business talk was boring you. We can go back to talking about relationships we've had or whatever else you like."

Scowling at him, I snap, "Just because I'm a girl doesn't mean I can't enjoy a conversation about business!"

Miles flinches, some of the color draining from his face, and I think some people at nearby tables heard me shouting and are disgusted with me.

"I'm sorry. I didn't mean it like that," Miles says, blabbering now. "I meant I'm happy to talk about anything you like."

when there could be someone slipping through the crowd at any moment to lay a hand on me. No offense to Miles, but he's not the scare-people-away type. He's more charming and likely to rescue you from being overbilled for your tax return.

"It's too bad they don't serve drinks here. At least the girls are going out after work. I think I'm done. Come on," I say, even though there's a little of my arepa left. But I've lost my appetite both for food and conversation and need to find a way to get out of here.

Miles gets up abruptly and nearly trips in a rush to follow after me as I grab my plate and leave. If I didn't know any better, I'd say I hooked his attention somehow, but I don't have the foggiest idea how.

Maybe he's into nerdy girls who've suffered blunt force trauma to the face. It's also possible he likes that I tell him what to do. But it's too bad for him that my current circumstances don't allow for a plus one, and no matter how good he seems, I can't completely rule out the possibility that he has a dark side.

The last thing I need is a guy who seems nice and sweet but can't wait to get me alone so that he can choke the life out of me. I already have one of those, I think, glancing around the busy food court to see if I can spot my mystery stalker.

We dump our plates at the receptacle and turn away toward the doors leading into the Bedrock building. I glance at the clock above the sliding doors and see that it's nearing 1 PM.

So much for my luxuriously long lunch. There are many more people around in the vicinity of the elevators as people return to their offices.

"You're heading back to work? A second ago I thought you were saying we should run for the hills to get away from this place," Miles says, struggling to keep up.

I stop abruptly and turn to him. He nearly collides with me.

usually this prickly. Or at least I don't think I am.

"Correction. I said *you* should run for the hills so you don't get corrupted. Me? I need to get back to work so I can find a way through this."

What I can't tell him is that there would have been a fairly good chance I would've happily skedaddled now that I had my check back, but that all changed when this new threat emerged. I'll pass on turning the corner only to be dragged into an alley. Here in Dallas, knives aren't the weapon of choice like they seem to be in Hochatown. Here, I'd expect a gun to my head.

Miles sighs dejectedly, but I don't have time for his disappointment and move toward the elevators when they open up. A herd of people move into the tiny metal box, and Miles and I are barely able to squeeze in as the doors close an inch away from our faces.

We're jammed in shoulder to shoulder, so close that I feel his warmth pressing against me. I see his reflection in the stainless steel elevator door as we go up, and for a moment there's a little tinge in my heart seeing his happy-go-lucky aura deflated, but I've got my own problems.

"Look, I'm sorry. The truth is I'm not all that good with women. Clarkson is about ninety-five percent men."

My eyes bulge. Why is he talking about these things with me in an elevator packed with other people? As if I don't have enough to be embarrassed about. I'm not even angry about his insensitive comments. It's that I'm constantly feeling like I'm at the edge of a cliff with somebody poking me in the back.

I'm not sure what Miles was expecting. That when I said it was a lunch date we'd be laughing the whole time and then sneak off somewhere to make out? Sorry, but I'm not Taylor.

The elevator dings, and some people shove through us on their way out, raising my hackles even more. I can tell Miles is

college with mostly guys seems like a lame excuse anyway.

The elevator opens up onto the fourth floor, and Miles steps out but turns around on the floor to look back at me. A couple of other people slip by. I expect Miles to have a hangdog look, but he's looking at me carefully as if I'm the one who didn't measure up.

Maybe I didn't. He opened up to me, and all I did was shut him out like I do everyone else.

"You know what I want?" I say, trying not to sound too frustrated. "I want someone for once to let me be myself."

Miles doesn't make a face or spit out a quick response or judge me, and for a second it's like I've gotten what I wanted. Then the doors close, blocking me so that I can't see his mussed hair, thin face, or shapely brown eyes.

I exhale sharply against the stainless steel door as the elevator takes me up. There are fewer people in with me now going this high, and I glance over my shoulder half expecting the stalker in the black windbreaker to be there. But there's no one, and the doors open to the sixth floor, where I step out to meet the rest of my problems.

The FBI agents are nowhere to be seen, and right now everything around the office appears to be perfectly normal. Did they figure out that Bedrock attempted to compel an employee to kill another employee and then hit the road?

But with so many floors, they could be anywhere.

I walk back to the HR office with my head held higher. All things considered, it was a good lunch date, and I know myself well enough that I can guess Miles will rattle around in my head for a while. He needs a little work, but I'm not perfect either, what with having killed one person, maimed another, and then assumed the identity of the deceased.

that have to wait for a second date.

Director Ron Zee is another story. As I approach the HR office, everything seems perfectly normal in there too. Through the windows, I can see that most people are at their desks, so whatever handling Zee insisted on may be all finished now.

Perhaps this whole FBI raid was much ado about nothing, making Zee's breathy warning to stay away as long as possible unnecessary. That would mean no one's here to bust the company for carrying out a hit or to take me into custody for performing it. Looks like I'm back to trying to figure out who wanted me dead in the first place.

I step inside the HR office and notice a barely detectible difference in the atmosphere. Janice and Shelley are still at their desks, typing away, but everyone is still on edge and hyperaware.

Janice glances at me out of the corner of her eye as I nonchalantly swing around behind her and take the seat at my desk. I set down my purse and take a moment to collect myself. Reaching into my pocket, I intend to confirm the check is still there, which it is, but mostly my hand lingers on the framed picture of me and my family.

The truth I can't admit to anyone is that somehow I want to go back to long before any of this started. I wish I could be a part of the loving family I thought I had before the car accident tore my sister Melanie away and pushed my parents into such a dark place that it earned them long prison sentences.

It takes me a moment to snap out of my painful personal reverie to realize that Janice has turned to me and is giving me a quizzical look.

I widen my eyes and shake my head at her. Like, "What?"

She purses her lips, sets her elbow on the desk, and leans in so that her dark curls drape over her arm. I don't know what the

pools in the pit of my stomach, right next to most of an arepa.

"To let you know," she says much slower than I would like, "while you were out, the federal agents came in here demanding to speak with you."

My blood runs cold.

"Oh."

9

Janice keeps watching me, but I don't know what she thinks she's going to find on my face. Regardless of what I look like or who I'm pretending to be, I'm not a young girl who's going to break down crying if I get pulled over going five miles above the speed limit.

I'm going to face this head on, but it would help if I knew more about what exactly I was up against. I want to find out what they know and suspect so I can get out of this. A lawyer might help, as if any lawyer in the universe would take my case if they knew the first thing about me.

"What did they say?" I ask, watching Janice closely and noticing the contrast between her dark curls and bright-blue eyes. Genetics is weird.

She scowls at me as if surprised by the question, straightening up. Whatever compelled her to whisper in the first place has vanished.

"They said you need to speak with them. They've taken over an office on the seventh floor by the bathrooms."

I recall the floor above us is for account management and IT, not that I've ever been there.

talk about?"

Janice smirks, sensing my discomfort. It feels like I'm about to become a new gossip thread on the Slack channel the moment I step away.

"And why would they give me that information?"

I don't have an answer for that but don't need one when Shelley suddenly speaks up from the bank of desks behind us.

"Did you see that one agent? Hoo boy, what a stud. I can think of something he can give me!"

Janice whirls around in her chair.

"Shelley! You know the rules. No swooning in the office!"

"Ugh, crud. I always forget about that one."

My eyes shift back and forth between the two of them until I conclude no additional information is forthcoming. Other than where to go, I'm left with no choice but to accept the obvious conclusion that they want to talk to me about the death of Emily Marks, the poor soul whose company set out to kill her, apparently simply for having the gall to show up for work for a couple of weeks.

I pick up my purse, a flash of nerves washing over me. Am I really about to do this?

"Righto," I say weirdly, since that's not something I say. "I suppose I'll go...and talk to them."

Still unsure, I rise slowly from my seat and stand there awkwardly for a moment above all the people around who are still in their chairs. I glance off to the side and happen to see Director Ron Zee leaning over a desk with another man beside him. I'm not exactly sure who the other man is, but he appears to be upper management and is talking urgently.

I lock eyes with Zee for a moment, which I wish hadn't happened. Now I'm feeling more on edge, and that's before he

can't break away from his current discussion.

"You know what to do."

I freeze, unable to nod or turn away, but Zee's attention is forced back to the papers on the desk and the ranting executive.

Without needing to say anything more, he's brought back everything he said in our uncomfortable encounter in the hall. He expects me to take the fall to protect the company. In his mind, I should admit to murdering myself to make the problem go away so this business can keep raking in cash while mocking its employees and customers in private online channels.

I step out of the office, and my instincts to run are competing hard with my desire to confront this head on. What's scarier, the FBI or a suspicious person in a crowd who seems intent to come after me?

Normally I'd say the FBI is scarier, but I recall not having a good time when a guy still on the loose promised to rape my dead body. Would not recommend. At least the FBI has rules, theoretically, right? One would expect to be safe. I unexpectedly wonder what Miles would think. Maybe he'd have some ideas, but I doubt being wanted by the FBI is a great look for a girl like me.

Leaving the HR office and again taking the trek across the wide floorspace to the elevator, I can keep my head up this time. I've already been found, and there's no use skulking along below the cubicle walls. The lunchtime traffic has cleared away from the elevators as well, and I only need to wait a moment before I'm riding up to the seventh floor.

Surprisingly, the seventh floor looks quite a bit different from the others. The hallways are narrow and covered in dark tile, bright lights overhead casting a harsh glare. This doesn't even feel like I'm in the same building, and the signs point to

around for a while without a clue where to go.

I pass some windowed conference rooms where I can see presentations being given featuring brightly colored graphics to rapt employees. Farther on, I see some computer infrastructure and what I have to assume are network managers keeping the company's operations running.

Feeling out of place among all this, it's almost a relief when I turn a corner and see a large man standing squarely in the middle of the hallway, the bright lights shining on his navy jacket with the large yellow letters.

There's no room to shy back or slink away now, and I stalk forward with as much momentum as I can muster. As I get closer, I can see the dark glasses covering his eyes but also notice his chiseled jaw and buff upper body.

Even closer, I notice what appears to be a spiderweb tattoo poking out from under his collar. He bends his arm and whispers into a mic on his sleeve, partially revealing what I think is another tattoo on his forearm of a knife up his sleeve. A buzzcut and a jutting chin complete the look.

As best I can tell, the FBI is hiring some tough guys these days.

He shifts his attention to me now that I'm standing right in front of him. There are doors on each side, and not far behind him are the bathrooms, a drinking fountain in between them. It's quiet and uncomfortable here. My heart rate won't go back to normal.

It feels like I'm making a big mistake, but I can't tell what I'm doing that's wrong. I need to make a big move, be confident, and...

"Are you Alice Patterson?"

...and perhaps not lie to the FBI, which would surely get me

prod at my back as I'm standing on the edge of the cliff. Some things are going to come out that need to be said.

"No."

10

This rough-around-the-edges FBI agent raises his eyebrow but doesn't say anything. Slowly, he leans to his right and opens the door, gesturing for me to go inside.

My nerves aren't calming down, and I don't have any other choice after coming all this way. If the FBI wants to talk to me, the only thing I can do is comply.

When I step in the room, I see that it's vacant except for a flimsy folding table and a pair of chairs. No windows, simple light-blue carpeting, and white ceiling tiles with the little holes.

While I'm looking around, the door closes behind me, and I hear the lock click. Instinctively, I lunge for the knob and try to turn it, only for my hand to slip without it budging.

"Did you mean to lock me in here? What's going on?" I yell right up against the door.

Granted, I don't have a lot of experience about how the FBI does things, but I'm starting to regret my decision to go along with this pretty quickly.

"One minute and the agent will be right in to speak with you," says the one who'd let me in.

Gritting my teeth and feeling trapped, I turn away and stalk

facing the door and decide to wait. Arms crossed and in a huff, I think about how to use this situation to my advantage. Whoever comes in is going to get an earful, and I will not accept for a minute that this is my fault.

Alice and Taylor had attacked me after all I wanted to do was have a fun weekend and make friends. Little details like who pushed the blade of a knife into whose chest are irrelevant considering this whole thing was engineered by the company we're smack in the center of.

A minute passes, then five. This is starting to feel like that one time in my life when I went to a dentist and had to wait.

I wish I'd gotten more information. If I knew who was behind this, I'm sure the FBI would be more inclined to take what I have to say seriously. The best I can do is point to the check in my pocket as proof, even though it could easily be a bonus check for anything. There's no memo saying, "For murder for hire" on it.

Thirty minutes pass, and I'm starting to lose my mind.

"Is someone coming to talk to me?"

There's no response, and I wonder if this is some kind of mind game. Have I basically been kidnapped by coming in here? The door is still locked, and I return to my seat, my discomfort growing.

In the privacy of this room, I take out the picture of my family. The sad thing is I only put it on my desk to make it seem like I have a life, but this ordeal has really made me miss the way things were, if only for an instant.

My mom, Diedre, has sandy-blonde hair like me and Melanie. Dad's black hair is neat and crisp. My sister and I are in blue-checkered dresses that look like they could be tablecloths, and Melanie is waving a TV remote like a magic wand.

I know in my heart that this singular moment is an anomaly

imagine it really meant something at the time and could again. Instead of a happy family, I have a ten-thousand-dollar check. The trade doesn't seem worth it.

Ten minutes later, I'm banging on the door, ready to tear my hair out.

"Let me out of here! I have to go to the bathroom! I need to take my medication! Hello, is anybody there?"

I holler and kick the door until I'm hoarse and my toes hurt, leaving me to sit back down and pull out Alice's phone. If it were my phone, it's possible I could call some people to at least talk, but the guy from the bar stole my phone and crushed it while he was stalking me at the lake.

Alice's phone has a few work numbers, and I consider calling someone to save me, but I don't think anyone's going to be receptive to voluntarily getting involved where the FBI is concerned.

Another twenty minutes later, I'm not even in the hard chair anymore. It's been a full hour of waiting, and I've reduced myself to sitting on the floor against the wall in the corner. Has sensory deprivation set in? It feels like the room is spinning.

A click echoes when the door unlocks, and a middle-aged man in a FBI jacket enters. I'm momentarily stunned to see another human being, and I scramble to my feet and return to the chair at the table as if I'd been starved of human contact my whole life.

My eyes wash over the agent, who doesn't look me in the eye as he lumbers over with a manila folder. The vibe coming from him is definitely not wholesome dad. He's got dark stubble, a broken nose, and a thick forehead that may technically make him a Neanderthal.

He settles into his seat and props his elbows on the table. Hands clasped together under his chin, he stares blankly at me.

anyone who came in here, but now I'm feeling so mentally flum-
moxed that it's like my mind has been wiped.

The staring contest continues. He watches me closely, face
blank of all expression. My attempts to rouse him by nodding,
raising my eyebrows, or humming don't get anything out of him.

I think I'll make him wait a full hour like I did before I speak,
but about fifteen seconds later I crack like an egg.

"What is it that you want from me? I had to wait way too
long. This is inappropriate," I say, my voice still scratchy from
the shouting.

He doesn't rush to remove his hands from under his chin
and set them on the closed folder. His knuckles are hairy, and
the smell of tobacco is on the verge of making me retch. Between
him and the one with the tattoos in the hall, the FBI seems to be
full of rough ex-military guys these days.

"Are you ready to talk?" he asks, tilting his chin up.

No introduction, no pleasantries, that's the first thing he
says.

"I've been ready to talk for an hour. Why did you make me
wait?"

His lack of emotion isn't professionalism. It's indifference.

"Go ahead."

"What do you want me to talk about? What am I even here
for?"

His eyes wash over me, green and slightly bloodshot.

"Why do you think?" he asks, and I shrug.

"Why don't you tell me?"

He moistens his lips and continues staring impassively in my
direction, through me.

"Why don't you already know?"

"How would I know?"

I'm starting to space out, my mind fuzzy from an hour of

why we're talking like this. What is wrong with this guy?

"I think you know," he says.

"Know about what?" I shoot back.

"Are you trying to be difficult?"

"Are you trying to be cryptic?"

"What do you think?" he asks.

I lurch back in my seat, astounded and not sure if this guy is even human. I might be speaking to a computer program right now.

"I think you guys show up here out of the blue. None of our supervisors tell us anything. I'm called up to speak here with no information about why. I wait for an obscene amount of time, and you expect me to tell you things with no clue what you want."

I can't help but get worked up about it, but the agent who may be trying to break me down with some kind of manipulative mental tactics acts like every facial muscle he has is paralyzed.

After casting his eyes in my direction once more, he abruptly gets up from his seat and starts moving toward the door.

"I'll give you some time to think about it," he says, and I jump out of my seat and rush over to him.

"No, please don't go. You know I'm not being uncooperative. I only need to know what this is about. I've been trying to figure that out all day anyway. I might be able to help you fix the problem here if you'll only point me in the right direction."

I'm clutching his sleeve and pleading with him, wondering if he takes another step if I'll have to drop to my knees. He hasn't even asked me who I am.

But something of what I said has gotten his attention, and he blinks rapidly and turns back to me.

"So you do know?"

in circles again.

"Yes, I know. I mean, I know a lot of things, but I don't know what you want to know."

Admittedly, I'm ready to spill my guts. Of course there couldn't be a mysterious death at a lake where three employees are staying together without someone coming to investigate the employer. I keep imagining that if I play my cards right, Director Ron Zee will walk out of here in handcuffs, with his boss behind him, and his boss's boss behind them both, all the way up however far it goes to the person who thought my death was a good idea.

The agent turns to face me squarely. We're nearly equal height, but he's probably over twice my weight with all of it made up of muscle. His impassiveness is starting to scare me, like he doesn't feel emotions or something.

"Are you ready to tell me what you know about the unauthorized transactions?"

I flinch and lean back as if the thing he said is creating a bubble of weirdness between us.

"What?"

The FBI isn't here at all to talk about my death and seems to have no awareness whatsoever about it. This is all about an unauthorized transaction.

Really?

I could use a drink right around now.

11

M y vocal disbelief doesn't sway the agent at all, but he moves back to his seat, and I go ahead and take mine. My head is spinning, and I start to feel this intense pressure rising in my chest.

"So this is all about an unauthorized transaction?" I ask, suddenly feeling like it makes zero sense for me to be here at all. Shouldn't the FBI be more concerned with, you know, people killing each other at the behest of their employers?

"Yes, please proceed to tell me what you know about it."

My mouth gapes open. There's a check in my pocket, but it hasn't even been cashed yet. That can't possibly be what he's talking about. I'm so lost.

"I don't know anything about it. What makes you think I would?" I ask.

"Because you came here to talk about it."

"I came here because you told me to come. I'm not in charge of any transactions. I work in HR. Why did you want me to come here?"

He stares at me for a moment, and I get an inkling for the

right.

"Because we're speaking to people from each department," he mutters, his voice growly.

"And why did you pick me?" I raise my hands, palms up.

"Because no one else in your department wanted to talk to us."

I pause for a moment, stunned, but then I start cracking up. The laughter keeps increasing until my face is red and pressed against the tabletop because I'm no longer able to control my body. It's too much, and I think back to Janice whispering insistently to put the fear of God in me about the FBI's demands for an interrogation.

"Let me... Let me get this straight. You went into the HR office, asked for a volunteer, and everybody volunteered the one person who wasn't there? Oh, they got me. I was out to lunch. That is so cold."

I'm laughing but crying as well now. As if I needed another reminder about the company I work for and what it deserves.

"Are you saying you have no knowledge of any unauthorized transactions?" he asks, and I shake my head.

"Absolutely zilch," I say.

He starts to get up again, but this time I'm ready and reach across the table to catch him by the sleeve and keep him seated.

"Excuse me," he says. The laughter has burned away, and only the revulsion remains.

"No, you're not leaving yet. I know you're here about a transaction, but that's not the real problem that's going on. You don't know what this company is up to or what's happened. I don't work for HR. I'm not even Alice Patterson!"

Whether it's what I said or the frantic look I'm giving him, some life comes into the agent's eyes.

that's the ticket I've been waiting for.

I lean forward on the edge of my seat. My eyes are so wide the information in my head could pour right out of them onto the table between us.

"You need to forget about whatever unauthorized transaction you're looking into. That doesn't matter. People within this company have hired an employee to murder another employee."

The agent's face scrunches up as if he smelled something awful. Although most of his face is pinkish, his nose becomes very white around where the break is, like all the blood has drained out of it.

"What are you talking about?"

I nod emphatically.

"My name is Emily Marks," I say, and it feels so good to say my own name, "and Bedrock hired me as a financial planner in early August. I worked here for a few weeks until last weekend when I took a trip with two other girls. One of them, Alice Patterson, was instructed by her boss to kill me."

"Someone tried to kill you?"

The agent looks at me warily, but I'm still trying to sell my story hard to him. He's asking the right questions now, and I can imagine the FBI taking over and sorting all of this out.

"Yes, someone in the company management above the HR director ordered Alice to try to kill me, which she waited all weekend to do until the very end. I don't know all of the company managers, vice presidents, and executives. You'll have to look into it. One of them wanted me dead."

The agent still looks like he had some bad tuna for lunch.

"Why would anybody want you dead?"

Exactly. The question gets me so excited I want to jump up and down on the table.

"That's the thing. I have no idea! I'm not in charge of

of special significance. I can't believe anyone in management above the financial services director even knew I existed."

The agent keeps eyeing me, and I'm beginning to gather that there's something dismissive to it. Either he's not sold on my story or thinks from my appearance that I'm not worth being bothered with. I don't particularly care about his opinion of how I look, but it would be nice if he could take in interest in who wants me dead.

"And where is Alice Patterson right now?" he asks.

I suppose that was an inevitable question, but it still makes me hesitant. I need to watch what I say carefully, because there are still some uncomfortable sides of this.

"Well, she attacked me and ended up dying. That's how I got this," I say, gesturing to my face. If there's a face that screams self-defense, it's this black-and-blue one plastered over my skull. "I believe right now she's in whatever morgue the McCurtain County Sheriff's Office uses."

I expect the agent to jump into action now that he's gotten all the information he needs, but instead he's chewing his cheek, leering at me in a way I wish he wouldn't.

"So you were in a fight with this girl Alice, and you ended up killing her?"

Despite his plain voice, the implication is clear that he thinks there's plenty of blame to go around between us.

"Actually, no, if you check with the McCurtain County Sheriff's Office, I'm sure they'll tell you that the third girl, Taylor Quince, had her fingerprints on the murder weapon."

The agent nods slowly, skeptically. My fervor is wearing off, and my current state is more like a cold sweat. I don't like that he isn't running with what I've already told him, like the dumb deputy did after I showed him Alice's fuzzy ID that looks a little like me.

I swallow. "Because they were both trying to get to me. Taylor was doing whatever Alice wanted, but it was dark, and she accidentally killed Alice with a knife while I was slipping away."

"Then how did you get such a big bruise?"

Trying not to cringe, I give the agent a pleading look.

"Because there was a guy who was after us, and he attacked me right after I left, but I got away from him too. Actually, it's good that we're talking about this, because I believe I saw him hanging around outside the building. He's still coming to get me, so if you could check around for a guy with one eye wearing a black windbreaker, that would be great."

He stares at me blankly, not getting right on that very important detail.

"Let me ask you this. If people at your job are trying to kill you, why would you show up to work today?" he asks, now chewing his tongue.

I'm growing exasperated and am breathing heavily. Why doesn't he understand and do something about it?

"Because I didn't know that until I showed up to work pretending to be Alice!"

My raised volume startles him a little, and he glances back at the door. I think he's going to try to leave again, but instead he crosses his arms over his chest.

"Let me see some ID now, please."

I chuckle lamely as I pull out Alice's card wallet in Alice's purse to pull out her driver's license.

"You see, it's Alice's ID. This isn't me. My nose is a little different, and my eyes are a slightly darker shade. You can see. But I don't have any of my own ID, because if I brought it, somebody here might figure out who I am."

The agent glances at the license then back to me and then at

table and then slides it back in my direction. He nods amiably and even flashes a quick smile.

"OK, I see what's going on here," he says.

I sigh in relief, settling back in my seat. Finally.

He continues, "How stupid do you think I am?"

My eyes widen. "What? Not at all—"

"You expect me to believe a girl with your name died, but it's not you. That you had a fight with her but didn't kill her. That you're not responsible, but some unknown person in this company is. That the company actually wanted to kill you, but you show up to work anyway."

"Yes!" I shout, elated that he's finally got it, but then his eyebrows drop.

"I've heard some outlandish excuses in my time, but that's something. Don't you think it's more likely you had a fight with this girl and killed her yourself, that the reason you have the ID of Alice Patterson is because you are Alice Patterson, that you don't know who in the company is involved because no one else is involved, and that you came to work because you thought everything was fine and that you could get away with it?"

"No, no, no!" I shout, my mouth suddenly dry. "That's not it at all. I'm Emily Marks. She's not dead. They're trying to kill me. Please!"

The agent is shaking his head, and I can tell I've lost him.

"Let me ask you one more question."

"Anything. I'm telling the truth. I swear it!" I say, my eyes welling up.

"Why would you admit this to us?"

"I didn't... I'm not..." I say, but he's rising from his seat and moving quickly to the door. His back's to me, and I'm trying to rush around the table, but my hip hurts from being in here, and I'm limping again. "It's the truth. They're trying to kill me!"

pulling it shut behind him. I flop against the side of it, distraught and in disbelief. Won't they look into it and know I'm telling the truth? Why didn't I keep my mouth shut and try to find out who did this to me on my own?

When I think things can't get any worse, the lock on the door clicks.

12

I stare at the plain gray door in front of me, fully incensed, but it's not the door that's bothering me.

Before the court case and the verdict that sent my parents to prison, there was one point when the detectives were going to talk to me. My mother, with her shoulder-length hair curling out at the ends and opportunistic light-brown eyes, gave me the sage advice I should've remembered five minutes ago.

"Tell them the least amount possible, nod at their statements, say you don't know if they ask you anything, and get out of there as fast as you can."

Instead, I went out of my way to implicate myself in a murder I'd gotten away with and now am trapped while they figure out what to do with me.

These four walls feel like they're closing in, and I refuse to spend another hour in this sensory deprivation tank, slowly losing my mind.

Alice Patterson might wait here demurely for the FBI to come back and arrest her, but Emily Marks knows to do whatever it takes to get herself gone.

This room offers scarce opportunities to do that, considering

my escape path marked as clearly as a one-way street.

I pick up one of the folding chairs, set it on the table, and start climbing. All of these ceiling tiles have to be held up by something, and once I'm on top of the chair I start pushing at them.

Reaching up, I pop one out of place and slide it away, creating a nice big hole in the ceiling. Next, I begin testing my weight, finding a side that seems to be connected to a crossbeam. I'm able to hang from it without it feeling like the entire ceiling is going to crash down on me.

I'm more of a thighs and calves kind of girl, making the effort of pulling myself into the ceiling way tougher than it needs to be. Even standing on the seat of the chair and then stepping into the top of the back isn't enough to give me the leverage I need to pull my body over the edge.

Straining as I exert as much pressure as I can with my elbows on the crossbeam, I feel the chair start to wobble underneath me. It tips over, but at the very last second, I hop off of it, getting enough height to prop my rib cage over the lip.

Legs dangling in the air and chair toppled over onto the floor, I have to slowly wiggle and slide into the space above the ceiling. The hard edge presses uncomfortably against my rib cage, stomach, and hips, until I've squirmed far enough up to be able to roll a bit and pull my legs up.

Gasping for breath in the ceiling space, which I don't think is even two feet high, I complete my disappearing act by reaching over and sliding the ceiling tile back into place, which has the unpleasant side effect of shutting out most of the light I was using to see.

I'm used to crawling through the gutter, so crawling through the ceiling is a nice change of pace.

I start to squirm along the beam in this crawlspace of inde-

lots of dust. The phone's flashlight helps me see what's around me, but I still manage to immediately snag my hair on something. It feels like part of my scalp is being torn away.

"Ouch!" I say and quickly chide myself.

I could be over another room by now, and the last thing I need is to give anybody a clue that I'm up here. The FBI is all over this floor, and I wouldn't be eager to see any coworkers either after trying to blame the company for my murder.

What was it that Director Ron Zee said would happen if I didn't take the blame and keep the heat off the company? Oh yeah, he implied they'd try to kill me. If you don't succeed, try, try again, I guess.

After unhooking my hair and sliding as quietly as I can, I listen closely then try to tease up the edge of a ceiling tile to see where I am. It's another room, not a hall, and from what I can tell there are people working on computers with humming computer mainframes nearby. I keep going.

Trying to be quiet makes my progress slow. Hopefully the FBI is in as much a rush to come get me as they were the first time they put me in that room. It gives me time to think.

I need to get out of here, and I need to find out who in the company is behind this attempt on my life. It wouldn't hurt to figure out who around here knows who I really am, and it would be best to avoid the guy lurking around the ground floor hoping to help me into a body bag.

I'm crawling forward, the massive amount of dust making my face, throat, and tongue feel filmy, and my thoughts quickly get much less productive. I dissociate from my claustrophobic surroundings and let my mind drift to something more pleasurable.

Miles pops into my head, his soft skin, silky bed sheets, his lips against my neck. My thoughts start to get pretty dirty as I

wires. Yes, I'd have to take charge with him, but I imagine he'd like having his pants ripped off and getting thrown on the bed so I can jump on top of him.

Considering he went to a college where girls are practically an endangered species, it might take him a handful of times to really get the hang of it, but I would very patiently teach him some things that would blow his mind.

It occurs to me that there's probably a zero percent chance of any of that happening considering he's Mr. Truth and Honor and everything he knows about me is a lie. He won't mind that I've committed one little murder, done some aggravated identity theft, and am on the run from the FBI, right?

My knee cracks one of the ceiling tiles, which splits in half and sends me slipping into the hole. Cursing myself for getting too distracted, I'm flailing to get control of myself with one arm and leg waving in midair above an empty conference room.

The bits of broken ceiling tile have scattered all over the table, chairs, and floor, and I'm struggling as hard as I can to avoid falling after them. I manage to reach across to the next tile over, which gives me enough leverage to get back on the beam.

The urgency to keep moving hits me, especially now that I'm starting to leave a trail. Thank goodness this room was empty, because there aren't too many good excuses for skittering around like a mouse within the walls.

Going in a straight line hasn't served me too well, so with the help of the phone's flashlight I find a good place to hang a left, hoping that I can find a spot to drop into the hall and get to the elevator before any of these federal agents can find me.

Not only is it dark and dusty up here, but it's pretty hot as well, and I feel the sweat dripping from my brow and making my clothes stick to me. The dust is turning to sludge on my neck

more than a half an hour.

I find a good spot to peek into the room below, which when I lift up the tile appears to be somebody's office. There's a window overlooking Dallas, a nice desk, and one of those bobbing drinking bird toys on it next to a cup of water.

I'm about to move on, but then I freeze when I hear the door open, my finger stuck through the lifted tile. There's a sliver I can see through right in front of my eyes, and I catch sight of a pair of men stepping into the room before closing the door behind them.

One man is the tattooed FBI agent from the hallway, tall and handsome. I purse my lips. Shelley can have him. He looks like the kind of guy who only likes it from behind and has a weird thing for feet anyway.

The other is a smidge shorter and hasn't stepped as far into the room, making it impossible for me to see anything other than some brown hair with gray strands interspersed.

"What's the problem now?" the executive asks, aggrieved.

A pregnant pause follows, and I try to stretch a little closer but still can't see any more.

"This girl has escaped," the agent responds.

I'm afraid to even smirk in case I'm detected up here, but I find that way of describing it to be hilarious. Either the agent isn't completely sure how I left the room or is too embarrassed about it to give more than a vague response.

The Bedrock guy groans loudly.

"What? Is this a joke? My wife is going to kill me."

"We're doing everything we can to find her. She can't have gone far. If you can get any information or assistance, that would be greatly appreciated," the agent says.

"Yes, of course. I'll let the staff know to keep an eye out for her."

me. Now the entire Bedrock staff is going to be in on my search?

"I'm sure it won't be long until we get her back," the agent says, and I see a seedy grin cross his face that makes my stomach turn.

The Bedrock exec had been shaking his head, but at that he jerked to the agent.

"Good, because if she's not, Emily could ruin everything!"

13

The two men storm from the room, and I'm left there to lower the ceiling tile and gape in the darkness at what I heard.

That executive knows my name, I think, but is he the one who stuck that ominous note on my computer mouse? There's no way to know for sure, but it's strange because I have no idea who this guy is or how he's even aware of my existence. Maybe the FBI agents already told him who I am after I revealed myself to them.

And why would his wife care? My head is spinning.

The thing that hits me the hardest is the last thing he said. I could ruin everything. How? What? He can't be talking about my attempted murder, because that already happened. What is going on that I could possibly ruin?

I don't think it's my attempt to expose the company for their murder-for-hire scheme, although based on what I heard, I have a good sense that this guy is not only involved but may be the guy who came up with it. Something else is happening here that I'm somehow a part of even though it's completely over my head.

all I know about him is the sound of his voice and what the top of his head looks like.

The temptation hits me to drop down right here and start looking into him, but what if they come back? Getting back into the ceiling doesn't look easy from here, and walking out into the hallway would be tantamount to leaping into the FBI agent's arms.

Even if I don't run into the FBI, now that the exec has put me on blast, the entire staff could be hunting for me.

I start crawling away, sick to death of being sandwiched in this ceiling crawlspace. It's disgusting and makes me feel filthier than I've ever felt in my life. Following the crossbeams, I slink on toward what I believe is the back of the building on the opposite side from my holding room and the FBI agents.

It's taken an ungodly amount of time to get here, and my phone is nearly out of battery, but I have no choice but to climb down into the hallway and hope for the best. Scaling down the elevator shaft is not an option. This isn't *Mission Impossible* or anything.

After sticking my head out to check where I am and make sure the coast is clear, I awkwardly try to lower myself off of the beam to the floor, but my lack of upper body strength leaves me unable to hold my grip, and I drop like a rock.

I come down hard on my ankle and flop sideways onto my hip until I'm sprawled on the hallway floor. The stinging is immediate, and many of my old injuries flare up again as well. A glance at my ankle doesn't tell me much, but when I try to get up it screams like a banshee. Great.

As I glare at yet another body part managing to be horrendously wounded, I hear footsteps coming from around the corner and have to get out of here. Pressing open the nearby

that the door closes quietly behind me.

It's a sterile space with poor lighting, and I gaze down through the middle to the very bottom without getting the sense that anyone else is in here.

I want to start getting my revenge on the nameless exec, my slimeball boss Director Ron Zee, and even all of the other people in the HR office who thought it was such a good idea for me to meet up with the FBI...

There's nothing to do about them now, and I have to start down the stairs and get out of here. If they're all afraid I'll escape and ruin whatever they have going on, they should know that's exactly what I'll do.

It would help if I know what it is and how to mess it up though.

Relying heavily on my good left leg, I trundle down the stairs with plenty of cringing and teeth sucking. I think I saw some Tylenol at Alice's desk, but I doubt I could make it back there. Too risky.

Instead, I carefully duck out of the hallway at the fifth floor, one where the fewest possible people are likely to be familiar with me or Alice, and barge into the nearby bathroom. There's a lady in one of the stalls, and I close myself in the other one until she's gone.

When the bathroom is vacant except for myself, I step out and look in the mirror above the sink to see the nightmarish sight that I've become. Yes, I need to clean myself up before I try to flee the building, because with the way I look, everyone will know something is up with me.

Dust is covering me from head to toe, making my hair look slimy and dark. It's curled around my collarbone and my ears. There are sweaty streaks of it on my face. My hands look soaked in grime.

which was sweltering in the heat and now looks like a giant dust bunny. Once over my head, it goes right in the trash, leaving me in a sheer undershirt tank top with spaghetti straps.

This would not fly on Casual Friday. Maybe Trampy Tuesday.

Either way, it feels like half of my Alice disguise is now gone without that shapeless hunk of fabric wrapped around my body.

I crank the sink's warm water and get to work washing the slimy grit off of my face, throat, and chest. The water keeps pouring out of the faucet, and I keep rinsing myself until even the sink looks like a dust bomb exploded on it.

My pants and top get pretty wet in the process, and once I've done the best I can to make myself appear like a human and not a sludge monster, I have to awkwardly stand under the hand dryer so that my shirt doesn't look soaked.

The last touch is to pull some concealer out of my purse and begin to apply it to my bruise, which is a beacon everyone would be looking for. Some makeup will go a long way to being less instantly recognizable, even if my extremely sensitive skin screams like I'm rubbing sandpaper on it.

It's not completely gone, but I think someone would have to be relatively close and really focus on it to see the extent to which a large section of my head was nearly blown off.

Taking a deep breath, I prepare to duck out of the bathroom and resume my escape from the building, hopefully managing to get through without the FBI or vigilante coworkers catching me.

I push the door open and slip back into the stairwell, but this time I'm not so lucky to find it completely vacated. It's getting late in the afternoon, and I see a guy in a suit carrying a briefcase as he hustles down the stairs.

He trots right down to my landing as I step into the stairwell,

beady blue eyes. The recognition is there. He knows who I am and that he should do something about it. I can see his mouth twitch as he's about to call me out, but I beat him to it.

"Heading home early?" I ask, a hard edge to my voice and eyes locked on his.

His eyes widen, busted and suddenly reticent. He does what he should've done in the first place, mind his own beeswax. Turning away, he continues down the stairs, and I follow right behind him, both to get going out of here as fast as I can and also to make sure he doesn't do something like turn onto one of the floors to rat me out.

We make it to the bottom without him looking back at me once, and then we continue through the doors into the main concourse. Now that the guy who caught me is striding for the exit, I let him go and focus on trying to slip through the doors in the distance without incident.

The expansive lobby space isn't as busy as it was during lunch, making it harder for me to get across it without being seen. I skirt the walls and huddle behind a large potted plant for cover, trying to see if there are any agents around I should be concerned about.

There are telltale black SUVs parked along the front of the building, but I don't see anyone lingering around with jackets, earpieces, or a suspicious posture like they're on the lookout for me.

Trying to sneak through the food court would only put me in the path of more people, and I'm not familiar with any back doors in this building. All I need to do is take a straight shot to the doors, get onto the street, and keep walking away.

But there are people hanging around, and I wonder if they'd spot me and try to hold me up. If I sprinted past everyone, what could they really do? But anyone in those vans

speed.

Breathing deeply, I psych myself up for a serious power walk, and then I see something outside the doors in the yellow afternoon sunlight. A truck pulls up with an office supplies logo, and I find myself nodding absently. This is my chance.

I hang tight for a minute as I watch the truck back up in front of the SUVs, open the rear, and begin to unload stacks of cardboard boxes. A handful of guys are there with hand trucks and low-platform carts ready to haul in all of these boxes, and my plan is to slip out while they're filing in.

The taste of freedom is so close.

When they start to move, I go around the side of the potted plant and double-time it to the bank of doorways stretching along the front of the building. I keep my head down and my feet moving, expecting at any moment that someone will shout one of my names.

But there's nothing other than idle chatter and the usual movement of those edging toward the doors right before quitting time. I keep moving, picking up the pace even as I pass couches and the building directory.

The deliverymen are opening the doors and wheeling in the boxes, and my hands are tingling with the realization that this nightmarish day is almost over. One of the deliverymen notices me zooming closer and extends his heel to keep the door propped for my exit. So nice.

My arm instinctively rises to catch the door so I can blow past and escape, but instead right as I'm passing the line of deliverymen, something suddenly appears in my peripheral vision.

The dark figure swoops in, and the next thing I know, there's a hand clamping down on my raised wrist.

It's such a blur that I can barely make out sleek black windbreaker before I'm jerking away, trying to wrench free.

making it impossible to hear him.

I'm fighting in the direction of the doors, trying to get away from my creepy stalker, who may be the guy who tried to kill me by the lake, but everything is happening so fast, and I try to fight my way forward.

He's behind me, and I feel his other arm wrapping around me across my chest, preventing me from moving another inch.

I can't move.

14

Whenn I think things can't get any worse with someone again grabbing me from behind, making my sore throat and chest hurt, things get much worse.

The black SUVs in front of me aren't empty, and the passenger doors swing open. A couple of agents climb out and come marching in my direction. Suddenly I don't want to go outside anymore, but getting away is impossible with someone struggling to keep me apprehended.

"Hey, hands off, pal!" one of the deliverymen shouts, seeing what's happening to me and stepping over to intercede.

I could kiss him, but I don't have a free second and have to make a run for it. The guy in the brown uniform with the bushy mustache is right in front of me, fending off my assailant. The FBI agents have reached the doors, which are only a few feet away.

As soon as I feel the grip on my chest and wrist loosen, I slip away between the two of them and dart in the opposite direction, weaving between the stacks of boxes back into the building. My injured ankle hurts, but I accept the pain and figure it'll have to be amputated later.

from everyone. I weave around the other deliverymen pushing stacks of boxes on their carts and then take off as fast as my amazingly toned legs can carry me.

The footsteps behind me motivate me to keep going, to sprint across the ground-floor concourse on my toes to get as much distance from them as I can.

"Emily!" someone shouts, but I'm moving so fast I can barely hear it, and I'm not stopping for anything.

Everyone else is so stunned that they don't try to get in my way at all, leaving me a clear shot to the stairwell. My momentum nearly causes me to smack into the wall, but I yank the door open and hit the stairs running. Up and up and up.

I don't have a plan other than evading my pursuers, but as long as I can keep flying up the stairs, I have a moment to think. Where can I be safe? Where won't they find me? Having only worked at Bedrock for a few weeks, my list of hiding places is very short. And it's not like crawling into the ceiling again is going to happen.

The footsteps are still behind me, echoing up the stairwell, but I don't know if it's my creepy stalker, the FBI agents, or both having a sick footrace to chase me down.

By the third or fourth floors, my legs start to give out, making me regret talking up my thighs and calves. Both are flagging, leaving me plodding up the stairs and sucking wind hard. The flights seem longer, and I begin using the railing to pull myself up.

By the fifth floor, the only thing keeping me going is the firm belief that slowing down will result in me being dead, for real this time, or sent to jail for life. The sixth floor doesn't come a moment too soon, and with a fleeting glance over my shoulder, I figure I've bought myself a few steps that I can use to get out of sight.

day, but instead of going straight to the HR office, I take a hard right in the direction of the bathrooms. I pass the women's room and shoulder the door to the men's room.

There's a young guy in there washing his hands, and he blinks hard when he sees me, stunned. I look at him like I would if I'd discovered a wart on my foot.

Grimacing, I shout, "What are you doing here? This is the ladies' room!"

He pales and jerks his head around to the urinals.

"I think—"

"Hey, I have to piss like a racehorse. Get out!"

My shouting hounds him out of the bathroom, but I doubt I'll be able to terrify any of the guys who are chasing me as easily. Clutching the sink and looking into the mirror, I struggle to catch my breath and give my tired legs a chance to recover.

Hiding in the men's bathroom seemed like a stroke of genius when I was hoofing it up those interminable stairs, but now I'm not so sure it's enough. I need to think of something better that would really take the heat off me, but I don't have many options to work with.

I snicker audibly about starting a fire somewhere in the office to distract everyone enough for me to slip out, but then I give myself an intense look in the mirror as I realize I don't have to actually have a fire to create a diversion.

In fact, right outside the bathrooms I saw the very thing I'm looking for.

Pausing as I hold the door handle, I hope I can do this fast and that nobody hunting me down is right on the other side of the door.

Pulling it open and slipping through, I lunge to the left and yank down on the lever in the little red box, retreating to the bathroom a half a second later.

off. I know I'm in deep and that doing a bad thing like this is only digging deeper, but it's really their fault for coming after me in the first place.

I can hear voices and footsteps as everyone on the floor stampedes to the stairs to escape the pounding noise, but I have to suck it up and stay in the bathroom, counting to sixty inside my head.

The agents and the guy in the black jacket would assume I've slipped into the crowd in the hope of disappearing inside the sea of humanity exiting the building in a calm and orderly fashion. They will be scanning every face that comes down the stairs, waiting to catch me.

But that's not my plan at all. Once I've finished my counting, I step out of the bathroom to find the floor completed vacated—no coworkers, no agents, no rogue killers, no one. But I do see the clock on the wall saying it's 4:50 PM. That means nobody who works here will be coming back in at all.

Having this huge space to myself feels luxurious and empowering, and as I traipse down the aisle between the cubicles, I'm tempted to dance to the music I've put on. But between my tired legs and many injuries from ankle to face, I settle for a steady power walk all the way to the HR section of the floor.

Like everywhere, I have the place to myself, and I gaze around the long bank of desks along both walls as I retrace my steps from the beginning of the day. The alarm is making my ears ache, but there's a yearning in my heart that can't be denied.

So many wrongs have been committed against me, and I have only a short time to do what I can to set them right.

Director Ron Zee's office is ahead of me along the hall, and it's even conveniently ajar, as if he left in a hurry for some reason.

The bonus check is still in my pocket, but the fury I have for

in the hall when I was pressed against the wall. The threat to have me killed next. His expectation that I'd go to jail for him and the company. The actual attempt to kill me that had me fighting for my life in Hochatown.

Zee may not have been the exec I'd heard on the seventh floor who orchestrated it, but the director carried it out with relish.

Slipping inside without even bothering to close the door, I admire his nice and clean office for a moment. His desk is a beauty, and I pull open that top drawer to find the bottle of whiskey he'd been sipping as the day began.

It feels heavy in my hand as I test its weight, roughly half-full. I slowly unscrew the cap and take a sniff, setting my hand on the back of his desk chair.

Holding the bottle out in front of me, I twist my wrist enough to start spilling the amber-colored liquid on the keyboard and desk. Next I pour some into the computer monitor. It takes getting down on my hands and knees, but I dump the rest into his desktop computer tower through the fan vent.

Now the whole room smells delicious, but I still have this empty liquor bottle. Winding up, I pitch it at the window across the room to the left of the door and watch the bottle smash to pieces. The window gets a nice big crack in it. There's glass all over the floor in the office and the hall.

Not done yet, I look at the sports equipment Zee keeps behind the desk. Picking the tennis racket up in both hands, I notice it has some nice heft to it too. I grit my teeth and raise it high over my head, slamming the frame against the top of the desk to create a dent. It takes a few more furious smashes to really dent the desk and break the racket frame.

This baseball bat is coming with me.

With no one anywhere around here, I'm free to do anything I

Slack channel, feeling safe that nothing would ever happen. And of course Zee didn't have a problem with the whole Bedrock staff getting trashed and tortured by the HR department.

The desks line the wall on both sides, and Alice's is in the middle on the left a few away from the door. I've worked up some adrenaline now from swinging that tennis racket, but I always had a soft spot for softball.

Taking a big swing, I hit a home run with Shelley's computer monitor for hazing me during my interview about black socks. Every single thing she said was a lie.

I smash anything that will break and clear off any papers and personal items until it's impossible to see the floor. Going from desk to desk to desk, I almost don't even notice it when I destroy Alice's as well. Janice's is the last to go, and I rip open her drawers and spill everything onto the floor.

The office looks like a war zone, and I lean on the bat and admire my work. If the Bedrock execs are worried about me ruining things, what else could I do but get started as soon as possible? Still, I think he was referring to something else, something bigger, but I don't know what he thinks I might get in the way of.

That makes me think of his voice, husky with a slow delivery, and I have a vague inkling that I may have heard it before.

I take a deep breath, glad I got my workout in for the day. Carelessly, I drop the bat onto the mess all over the floor for someone else to pick up.

The muscles in my arms and legs are tired from all of this exertion, and I stretch as I waltz out of the office back toward the stairwell.

Now I could really use a drink.

Where was everyone going for girls' night?

15

M y romp through the office complete, I reach the empty
stairwell with some pep in my step and an irrepressible
smile on my lips.

Having worked at Bedrock for most of a month, I'd never
once left with a sense of satisfaction like this. Perhaps that was
because I hadn't done any work before. Ransacking the office
with a baseball bat may not qualify either, but I don't see the
need to quibble.

On the stairs, I'm able to take them as comfortably as I need.
My right ankle is throbbing from my fall from the ceiling, so I
appreciate the lack of urgency and shift my weight to my left as
much as possible.

Now if only somebody would shut off the blaring alarm and
the flashing lights. These things are annoying.

I reach the ground floor feeling better than I did at the start,
perhaps because walking downstairs has spurred some blood
flow or something, and step off the stairs ready to tackle the next
part of my mission.

Getting some revenge on office furniture was nice, but the
people need to be held accountable too. Why do the people I

floor talking suspiciously with the FBI agent about me ruining something important?

Because no one is at work anymore now that my fire drill has booted everyone out, I'm going to have to find the answers outside of the office, and I don't have a minute to lose. Fortunately there's a spectacular opportunity to get answers happening at a gathering about to start, and sweet, colorful alcoholic drinks should go a long way to loosening some tongues.

I step out of the stairwell and see some tall figures in heavy jackets with bright-yellow reflective stripes. Immediately, I break into a pronounced limp as I lurch in their direction. If there's any dust remaining from crawling around in the ceiling, that's all for the better.

The three burly firemen slow down as they reach me, and I put on a good show of being winded and hurt, gasping and partially hunched over, looking up at these men who dutifully think they're here to fight a fire. At least they won't be putting their lives on the line today.

"I took so long because someone stomped on my ankle," I whine.

The firemen couldn't care less about my story and quickly leave me to continue with the task of resolving the situation.

Straightening up and walking more normally onward in the direction of the building's main entrance, I do feel bad about wasting their time, but I have to chalk it up to another consequence of this company not simply letting me do my job.

Unlike before, the ground-floor concourse is completely vacant, as is the adjoining food court. No one's watching where I go or running up to try to apprehend me or kidnap me. Some of the overhead lights have been turned off, leaving only the flashing fire alarm lights and the attractive glow of the light coming in through the building's front windows and doors.

my sins, and I stroll forward with every intention of leaving this place behind and never coming back. Emily is dead, and Alice has thoroughly burned this bridge, but I'm still here and have to keep fighting for my safety and livelihood.

There are still about one hundred people milling around in front of the building, but I don't see the SUVs or anyone in a black windbreaker around. I'm extremely confident as well that any email from management telling people to keep an eye out for me has slipped completely out of mind in the midst of this sudden mass exodus.

That means it's as easy as pie to simply nudge open the door and cruise on out into the warm early September air here in Dallas. As much as I'd like to take credit for getting everyone out of work early, no one pays me any attention, and I don't linger.

Instead, I hang a left and start down the sidewalk, my eyes searching for the most likely destination for this girls' night that somehow even Director Zee seemed to be aware of.

As inconspicuously as I can, I scan the area and scope out a few establishments in easy walking distance from the Bedrock office, because I'm sure they haven't gone far. There's one place across the street called Peabody's, but it seems too snooty.

A place called What the Crepe? has a cartoon character on the signage and seems to be a family-oriented place. I know for a fact neither Janice nor Shelley have any inclination to bring their families, if they have them, and even the way they spoke around the office was not family appropriate.

Craning my neck toward the street to get a better angle, I see that I'm approaching a bar at the end of the block called Three Tequila Floor. This was actually where Alice, Taylor, and I were originally planning to get together for happy hour before they decided they wanted to go to Hochatown to try to kill me instead.

the entrance, and country music filtering out from inside, I don't have a doubt in my mind that this is where Janice and Shelley are. They never told me who else they were inviting or how many would be here from the office, but I hope somebody can give me the answers I'm looking for.

All I have to hope for is that Director Zee isn't attempting to crash the girls' night or anything.

Stepping into the bar, I already feel so much more in my element. Stuffy offices with dress codes and the need for productivity are still things I have to get used to, but watering holes like this where I can say whatever comes to mind, flirt, and cause trouble fit me like a glove.

I check the bar but don't see anyone I recognize along the row of chairs, only some regulars with flannel shirts, boots, and the occasional cowboy hat. Nobody's playing darts. Some guys are hanging around outside a side entrance smoking cigars.

That leaves the tables, and I begin milling around the floor, which isn't nearly as sprawling as the office floor but has enough people in it that there's scarcely an open table or two among the thirty spread out from one end to the other. Looks like the workday causes plenty of people around here to drink on a Tuesday.

I'm roaming, wandering, trying not to bump into anybody else who's moving around, when I see a group of women seated at a table for six somewhere around the middle of the bar. Sure enough, another step forward shows me Janice's dark-brown curls and floral dress. Then I see Shelley, who has undone two of the buttons from her striped top and is raising a beer to her bright-red lips.

A sigh of relief follows. They're in my world now and will have to play by my rules. If everything goes according to plan, somehow at the end of it I'll have justice for myself and ten

until I can find another job.

Shelley, leaning back, notices my approach, and I brighten up as if I didn't destroy every personal item at her desk moments ago.

"Alice, you made it!" she says, waving me over with more enthusiasm than I would've expected. If anyone got or saw an email about me from the gruff seventh-floor exec, no one cares.

Janice twists around to look over her shoulder in surprise. "I can't believe you finally came for once."

I shrug. "If there's a day that calls for a drink, it's today," I say, though they don't know the half of it.

"That fire alarm scared the bejesus out of me," Shelley goes on. "I was in the middle of firing someone right before she retired at the end of the day. Maybe I shouldn't have waited until the last minute."

Petty laughter follows, and I force some out to go along with it, knowing I'll be having the last laugh when they go in to work tomorrow.

Standing beside Janice, I glance around the table at the other occupied chairs, one open for me. At the left end is another gal in her thirties like Shelley, this one plump with short blonde hair. Next to Shelley on the opposite side is a gaunt lady closer to Janice's age with her hair up, a wrinkly face calling out for Botox, and some bony fingers clutching a glass with nothing but ice left.

I start thinking that instead of a girls' night, I've intruded on more of a moms' club meeting, but then I catch sight of the one to my right with a dark-brown ponytail, Cowboys jersey, and skin a bit more tanned from some time at the beach.

She'd been quiet and didn't even look my way as I approached, but now that I've noticed her, she's startling me

has put her in a trance.

I crack a tepid smile and give her a half-hearted wave, thinking that getting the answers I want isn't likely to be nearly as easy as I thought it would be.

Not with her sitting next to me.

I can't believe it's Taylor.

16

"You going to stand there, or do you want to join us?" Janice asks, making me realize that I'm awkwardly having a mental breakdown as I try to figure out what to do because Taylor is here.

The last time I saw her was in the dark loft when she was plunging a knife into Alice's chest. I have no clue what happened to her after that. Apparently she wasn't picked up by the sheriff's office, made it back to Dallas from Hochatown, and came into work despite being wanted for murder.

Yeah, I'd told the sheriff's office the guy from the bar broke in and did it, but I figured they'd get Taylor from her prints on the knife. Or at least she wouldn't come into work because she lied to get her job too and was a scamming crook, but it looks like she called my bluff. I didn't report her, and Ron Zee isn't likely to care even if she's robbing banks.

"Of course. Sorry I'm late," I say, pulling out the vacant chair and taking a seat.

I glance casually at Taylor, who is still deathly silent and appears to be stewing. It's putting a major damper on my fun, but not everyone appears to be affected. Shelley leans forward in

brown ale.

"I know why it took you so long to get here," she says, eyeing me. "Look at you. Concealer on that bruise, and you got rid of that thick sweater. Between that and the kind of bulky tops you usually wear, I didn't know you actually had a body under there!"

I laugh, trying to skate over some embarrassment at being in my undershirt and showing a lot more skin than everyone else in their work clothes.

"Sometimes you've got to cut loose, right?" I ask, trying to own it.

Janice on my left eyes me up and down.

"If I didn't know any better, I'd say you were looking for a little action tonight," she says furtively.

"So what if I am?" I ask, playing along, even though I've got more important things to do than find a guy to pick up. Considering how that worked out for Taylor and Alice, I'm not in a rush to find another con artist like Wesley or the serial killer who followed me here from the woods of Oklahoma.

I spare a thought for my new crush, Miles, who I would've repulsed if he ever got to know me. Doubtful I'll see him, his messy hair, or his nice brown eyes ever again.

"Then that makes two of us!" laughs the big girl at the table's left end, raising a margarita and taking a sip. Her smile is infectious, and I get the impression she isn't blowing smoke.

Janice shakes her head at her.

"Gina, leave them boys alone. Some of these guys you've been talking to, you could be their mother," she says, and Gina raises her eyebrows with an affronted look.

"And what's wrong with that? Get 'em while they're young!"

It's easy to laugh along, even despite Taylor's continued sour glare. After a comment like that, the natural segue is to start

isn't done with me yet and eyes me carefully.

"Really though, Alice, we must've invited you out twenty times without you showing up. What made you come now?"

I run my hand through my hair from back to front, hoping some of it will fall in front of my eyes and make me appear more Alice-like. The last thing I need is for her to get suspicious and recall that she interviewed me a month ago and that I'm not who I say I am.

I sigh casually, glancing at the ceiling.

"After getting clocked in the face this weekend, it really woke me up that I need to live a little more, enjoy life before it's gone."

Shelley nods with gusto. "Words to live by!"

Janice leans in my direction, and I can feel her pressing against my shoulder.

"But what really happened to give you that wicked boo-boo? Looks like somebody tried to take a jackhammer to your cheek."

I jerk in her direction, surprised at how close her guess is, but that is a story they don't really need to hear.

"Let's say that our canoe paddling skills are in dire need of improvement," I say with a wry grin.

A sharp scoff and head shake to my right from Taylor ruins my moment, and I look over to see her rolling her eyes with disgust. An awkward silence ensues, and I start to get aggravated at the prospect of her ruining everything I say.

If this conversation doesn't get into a good rhythm, I'm never going to get the answers I want out of them.

Shelley notices Taylor's chilly demeanor and is about to say something when someone interrupts, approaching me from the side.

"Hey there, can I get y'all anything?" says a red-haired server with pigtails. She's got on cutoff jean shorts and a super-tight white t-shirt. The girl looks barely old enough to serve alcohol

running up each ear.

Considering this party has not gotten off on the right foot and needs a serious course correction before Taylor can derail it anymore, the answer for me is yes.

"Yeah, can I get another vodka on the rocks?" asks the lady across from me, Hope, shaking her glass full of ice.

A sudden hand on my shoulder startles me, and I'm surprised that it's the server, who's leaning on me for some reason while she takes our orders. When I give her a questioning look, she gives me a half-smile.

"What about you, darlin'?" she asks me, and I have to shudder at her twang before I can answer.

"How about a strawberry daiquiri, please?" I ask, turning away.

Shelley lights up. "Enough of the beer. I'll take one of those too."

The server chuckles like two people ordering the same drink has never happened here before.

"Vodka on the rocks and two strawberry daiquiris coming right up. I just need to see some ID," she says, and I realize she's talking to me again, even giving my shoulder a little squeeze.

It's been years since I was even close to twenty-one, so I look at her like she must be joking. Although she's standing there waiting, I'm still not buying it and turn to the rest of the group.

"Yeah right, I wish I was still under twenty-one!" I say to genuine laughs in the hope that she'll simply agree and scamper off, but instead she doesn't budge an inch.

"Come on. It's the law, hun," she says with good humor.

We could have an enlightening discussion about how much laws are really worth, but instead I see that I'm not getting out of this one and am going to have to cough up some ID to drink. I

wallet, making me start to second-guess myself.

It's unlikely Taylor knows the full extent to which I've tried to step into Alice's life, and I'm afraid that seeing me with her license will set her off on another tirade like when Wesley let it slip that I was a fraud at my job.

Slipping Alice's driver's license out, I extend my hand to the server with the card firmly concealed against my palm so that Taylor can't see.

"There you are. Perfectly legal," I say, waving the card in my palm past her before starting to retract it.

"Hold on a sec," the server says, snatching the ID out of my hand before I have time to react. She is quick on the draw, and I watch in dismay as she holds it up to her face and starts to read it.

That gives me time to read the name tag she's wearing, and my patience is wearing very thin for Shaylene. The delay has drawn the attention of everyone at the table.

"You new, sweetie? That ain't a fake," I say, able to give her a complete presentation on what fake IDs look like and how to get them.

Shaylene puts her hand on her hip and gives me a sidelong look. At least she's no longer clutching my shoulder, but she does squint at the ID and then glances at me and then back to the card. I start to feel pressure in my chest.

Meanwhile, Taylor leans back comfortably in her seat. Now she's having a good time and starting to relax while I squirm.

Shaylene raises an eyebrow at me.

"This doesn't really look like you, does it?"

Everyone is watching, and I'm holding it together as best I can. These girls aren't going to tell me anything if they think I'm here under false pretenses.

I scoff, talking to her but looking at the group from Bedrock.

favor and stay eighteen as long as you can."

There's some snickering from the ladies, and I practically start reaching up to take my license back.

"No, that's not it. I mean, you don't look the same. It says the eye color is hazel but yours are more brown."

I shake my head. "Probably some idiot at the DMV put it in wrong. I didn't even notice."

"But your nose is a little narrower, cheekbones a little higher."

My consternation keeps rising and starts to leak through. "Excuse me," I say, now glaring at her, "but if you must know, I lost a few pounds since then. This is getting out of hand."

I reach up to try to recover Alice's license, but Shaylene, standing, is able to easily move it out of reach. Taylor is covering her mouth to hide her laughter, and I'm wondering why this girl won't let it go so I can buy a drink. She could've taken five other orders by now.

"You lost a few pounds in your nose?" she asks, openly antagonizing me and glancing at the other girls to convey her incredulousness.

I'm beside myself. This is almost a tougher interrogation than the FBI agent with the broken nose earlier today.

"It's a bad picture, Shaylene," I say, crossing my arms.

Yes, we're doing this now. If she wants to keep bringing things up, I'll go all day fending off any insinuation that I might not be the girl in the picture who very much is not me.

"Alright, forget the picture," she says. "What's your address?"

I nearly gasp, my anxiety starting to rise. I start to wonder what she'd do if she found out the ID didn't really belong to me. Would she get a manager and call the cops? That's the last thing I need.

All I wanted to do was get a little wasted, and suddenly I'm

office have front row seats, looking varyingly puzzled and amused.

And of course I can't recall what Alice's address is for my life. I try to glance at the license, but she catches me peeking and slaps the card to her chest. Grr.

"Oh, that?" I say, blatantly stalling. "It's, um, it's Dugan Street. I mean, Duking Street. Something starting with a D. I can't remember the number. I just moved."

Shaylene checks the license and shakes her head. I'm probably not even close, and a sinking feeling starts to hit my gut. She's becoming increasingly suspicious, looming over me while I'm in this seat.

"Then what's your birthday?" she asks straight out, and an agonized sigh escapes me.

I feel the final nail being put in the coffin. After all I went through in Hochatown and around the office with Director Zee and the FBI, somehow I've been busted by this girl who is barely old enough to vote. I should've memorized the license. Such a bush-league mistake, another sign that I've gone soft.

My frustration gets the better of me, and I snap, "I can't remember anything now that you've gotten me flustered. When's your birthday?"

She looks me dead on. "You can't remember your own birthday?"

I wince and recoil, wondering if I'm going to have to bolt. The other girls are looking at me strangely, except for Taylor, who has a cocktail with a straw that she's sucking on with relish.

My mouth opens, but I'm not even sure what I'm going to say. I've run out of lies.

Shaylene's harsh glare cracks into a huge smile. She's laughing, nearly doubling over, her hand on my shoulder again.

"I really had you going, didn't I? Oh my goodness, wasn't that

the hot seat like that. I'll be back in a jiff with those drinks. I like to earn my tips, you know what I mean?" she says, giving me a glance before she drops the license on the table in front of me and saunters off.

I'm speechless. Everyone is looking at me with forced smiles, wondering what that was. This server nearly blows up the scheme I've staked my entire life on and desperately need in order to find out who's trying to kill me, and she expects me to tip her for it.

I exhale a wheezy breath, trying to keep myself from visibly shaking.

I don't want to make a habit of killing people, but that server has me contemplating murder.

17

"Thank you, Shaylene, if that is your real name," I say, giving the red-haired server a sidelong look and cheeky grin as she places my ruby-red daiquiri on a napkin right in front of me.

The other girls get the message. If I'm having fun, it must all be a joke and there's no reason to suspect that this teen booze peddler has unwittingly outed me in front of everyone. I mean, if Taylor can keep her big mouth shut, Shaylene should rein in the waitress antics.

"Bless your heart," she says in that sarcastic way, shrugging one shoulder and scooting away.

I breathe a sigh of relief once she's out of sight. My eyes fix on the shapely stemware glass in front of me, already beginning to get a little condensation on the outside from the warm air. Full to the brim with rum and strawberries, it has half a strawberry and a slice of lime perched at the top, a white straw poking out of the middle.

With a devilish grin, I savor the anticipation and slowly pick up the glass, feeling like I've waited all day for this. Once the

throat.

I needed that, I think, knowing right now I could see myself guzzling a handful of these. But I'd better take it easy. Even if it is Alice's money, I need to get answers before I get so drunk that I need to be carried out the door.

I set the glass back down, pacing myself before I chug the whole thing and go nuts until I need to have my stomach pumped. This isn't middle school.

"So, an FBI raid in the morning and the fire alarm in the afternoon," I say smoothly to the others, feeling more at ease already. "What'll we have tomorrow, an earthquake and tsunami?"

"We better not," Janice grumbles. "All these distractions meant I didn't get my report done and will have to do it first thing tomorrow."

"Me too," Shelley says. "If I don't compile these evaluation results, Director Zee is going to eat me for lunch, and not in a good way."

I take another heavenly sip. *Cheers*, I think to myself, imagining them walking into the office tomorrow in a rush to get to work. Now who's stupid and lazy?

"What was that even about with those agents coming into the office?" asks Gina, making me sit up. "They wanted all of these payment records and receipts."

"Worst day of work in my life."

That was Taylor, and I'm surprised when she makes an actual contribution to the conversation. She's sitting there glowering with her arms crossed, slightly haggard and on her second drink.

Since she's in the accounting department, I start to put together what she's been through. We had our fight together in Hochatown Sunday night, leaving Alice dead, then she came to

requests.

I don't know what happened to her in the middle, how she got from the cabin back to Dallas, but it doesn't look like it was all roses and daffodils.

"After being so nicely volunteered by the rest of my department to talk to them, I did learn some things," I say, putting that out there.

Janice and Shelley share a guilty look before Shelley waggles her head at me.

"Oh, it couldn't have been that bad. Being young like you, I bet they spent more time looking you up and down than asking you questions, baggy sweater and horrific bruise or not," she says.

I bite my tongue.

"Those agents cursed out my department head when he couldn't find some of the records," Gina went on. "Nasty, that's what they were."

I recall their tattoos and the one guy's broken nose. She's right.

Janice glances at me, and I know I've got her hooked. Taking another delicious sip of sweet red goodness, I wait patiently until she can't hold back anymore.

"OK, so what did you learn?" she asks.

I suck the straw one more time, set the glass back down, and rest my fingertips on the table.

"One thing they specifically asked me about was if I'd heard anything about a big unauthorized transaction. That's the whole reason they came. Something about money moving when it shouldn't have."

Glances abound as everyone processes that, washing it down with alcohol. I'm excited seeing the wheels turning in their heads. They don't need to know that someone in the office

point me in the right direction nonetheless.

"They took so many records and hard drives with them that everyone is terrified to even pay the company phone bill," Gina says, cringing.

In a lower voice that makes them all listen closer, I say, "As I was coming back, I happened to hear one of the agents talking to one of the executives on the seventh floor, a man maybe a little under six feet with some gray in his dark-brown hair. Does anyone know who has an office on that floor?"

Janice squints at me. "White, middle-aged, and male describes about ninety percent of the upper management."

I rack my brain, trying to remember more that might help them identify the one I'd heard while I was in the ceiling, but I have so little to go on.

"Umm, his voice is rich and deep with kind of a slow, emphatic speaking style."

The other ladies chew on that for a moment, Janice tapping her chin until she turns back to me.

"It might be Terry Glint. He's a vice president, one of the first with the company. I wouldn't be surprised if he was taking charge of Bedrock's response to the investigation."

I shrug as if it doesn't matter that much, but inside my excitement is building. If he's in charge of that, he might be in charge of knocking off a new financial planner as well, but why?

"He said that the company had some big new plan or deal or something that might be ruined. Do any of you know what he was talking about?"

I survey their blank faces and know I've struck out on that one. Maybe an answer to that was too much to ask for. Nobody here is in management.

That wrinkly lady across from me, Hope, scratches her head and leans toward me.

Q Fund hard. That's all Bedrock needs to make money."

I recall Miles mentioning that, and I had gotten the same message when I was pretending to be a financial planner. But there must be something going on. Terry Glint made it sound like it was going to be devastating if I ruined it. But what was he even talking about, and why would I be so involved that the only way to protect it is to kill me?

I'm thinking hard, my brain on overdrive, when a voice behind startles me.

"Who's ready for another?" Shaylene asks, and it feels like she's shouting it right beside my ear.

I grit my teeth. My daiquiri is still half-full, but if this server keeps getting on my nerves, I'll definitely need another quickly, though perhaps I'll go to the bar myself for it. I suppose she thinks she's being funny or cute, but I'm getting serious vibes from her overeagerness that remind me of Mr. Chambers, our Airbnb host.

"Can I get another summer ale?" Shelley asks, having demolished her own strawberry daiquiri. Someone is going to have to pour her into bed.

"Tequila sunrise," Taylor says, though she looks at me like she's expecting me to go get it for her.

Shaylene manages to leave without antagonizing me any further, which feels miraculous, and it's good because I'm not finished grilling my fake coworkers.

"There was one other thing he said that made me curious. He said something about his wife being really angry about it. Does anybody know who she is?"

Taylor snorts next to me, shifting in her seat.

"Thinking about sleeping your way to the top?"

My lips part, but Shelley jumps in quickly.

"Hey, I was going to say that!"

"No, but does anybody know? Why would somebody's wife care so much about Bedrock's new plan getting ruined by some-one?" I ask, leaving out how that someone is me.

More puzzled looks. Maybe I overestimated the value of getting anything out of this group. At least they knew the execu-tive's name, possibly, but they don't appear to be forthcoming about more.

Assuming they're willingly sharing everything they know.

"Maybe she's got some investments or is hoping he gets a big bonus," Gina said, and I nod grimly.

Her guess is as good as mine, but I recall the way the execu-tive lamented it. He made it sound like his wife was going to kill him over me getting loose. Once again, there's someone I'm completely oblivious to who wants to get very involved in my life for reasons I don't understand.

"They're all like that," Janice adds, shaking her head. "The upper management would happily turn the whole company into a sweatshop. I get having high expectations, but cut us some slack."

Her venting makes me want to bring up the Slack channel and how HR treats the rest of the staff like playthings, but instead her comment makes me think of something else.

"What about the CEO?" I ask.

"Candace Roberts?" Gina says, not concerned and slightly bobbing her head to the music. "She's very reclusive. Some say she even has her own entrance to the building, her own elevator. The rumor is she works at odd hours and doesn't interact with the rest of the staff at all except for a handful of VPs."

"Like Terry Glint?" I ask.

She shrugs. "Probably."

The question I want to ask is if whether the interest in my death goes all the way to the top, but it's hard to imagine

alone my hiring or some plot to kill me.

If I were the boss, the one thing I would definitely delegate would be the plans to kill employees. And maybe it's only because she's a woman, but I have to think being super rich and the leader of a powerful company would give her other priorities and interests other than what a dirt-poor new hire does with her life.

"Whatever it was about, everyone is going to be on pins and needles for a long time," Shelley adds, raising her eyes as I hear some footsteps behind me.

There's some movement behind me from more than Shaylene carrying drinks on a tray over to our table, and I glance over my shoulder in time to notice a group of guys passing through and crossing paths with her.

Shaylene, gritting her teeth, tries to squeeze through, but one of them bumps into her. Out of the corner of my eye, I see her take a lurching step, struggling to keep the tray level. Shelley's summer ale tips over, dumping beer right on my shoulder and back.

"Ahh!" I shout, the liquid feeling like an ice bath that immediately starts dribbling onto my chest and lower back. My arm is slimy, and it feels like I'm covered in a film as I attempt to hobble to my feet and shake some of it off my drenched arm.

Janice immediately grabs some napkins while most of the others gasp and watch. Wide-eyed, Shaylene is beside me, trying to dab me with a cloth from her waistband.

"I'm so sorry," she stammers, but I'm feeling grossed out and want some space more than anything.

After everything else she's put me through, and despite seeing her get bumped, a little part of me thinks she could've done something to keep me from getting soaked. Maybe I'm

wonder if this happened on purpose.

"Which way to the ladies' room?" I say, exasperated, and Shaylene points vaguely to the back corner.

Suddenly Taylor bursts from her chair, eagerly stepping toward me.

"I'll help you!" she says.

I freeze momentarily, considering how many lies I've heard from Taylor and what we've been through.

I'm dead certain the last thing she wants to give me is help.

18

W ith everyone at our table staring at us in the aftermath of the beer-splosion, I have no choice but to respond in kind.

"Oh, that's so nice, but I've got it," I say to Taylor, nodding.

"It's no trouble, really," she says, coming still closer.

I take a labored breath, beginning to grasp what she's after.

"It looks like your drink didn't spill. Go ahead and enjoy your tequila."

But Taylor's not stopping for anything, almost making me think she's ready to rush at me right here in the middle of the bar.

"Your top is staining and becoming a bit see-through," she says, pursing her lips. "Unless you want to try to win a contest, I've got another top under this jersey."

I look down and cringe at the sight of my side and waist visible straight through my shirt. Some of the polka dots on my bra are showing. Nice.

But being embarrassed is one thing, and being assaulted by a lunatic who'd tried to stab me to death more than once is

lethal thing in mine is some chapstick.

Taylor won't be denied though, and I don't see what I could possibly say in front of everyone to change the outcome here. If she wants to follow me to the bathroom, I don't have any way to stop her. The thought crosses my mind that I could simply leave now that I've gotten some new information, but she could simply follow me out too.

Being out on the streets with her might be worse.

I give her my game face and then turn for the bathroom between other tables, past other servers who seem to have much steadier hands than Shaylene, and past the kitchen, which gets my stomach rumbling. Is that barbecue chicken?

I shake my head, trying to get it back on track. Unless there's a party in the bathroom, I anticipate the confrontation we're going to have, trying to figure out what to do. She's already ruined my plans of being the life of this party with fun stories and jokes, but she did commiserate about a tough day's work complying with the FBI.

I wonder if she was nervous being around federal law enforcement while Alice's body is barely cold in a morgue. Was Taylor spending the entire day imagining her revenge against me and is now jumping at the first chance?

I still don't understand how she managed to get out of Hochatown at all.

The maroon bathroom doors are ahead of me, and I take the second one for women, stepping into the modestly sized facility with three sinks and as many stalls. At least it isn't a single bathroom jamming us together for our rematch.

I've already turned and have my hands up as she steps through the door, letting it close on its own behind her. Although there's a chance that someone might be in one of the stalls, my gut feeling is we're alone in here.

isn't looking as pretty as it did when we first rolled into Hocha-town. Her eyes are a bit red and puffy from fatigue, her ponytail is messy, and I doubt she's washed that jersey since wearing it often during the weekend.

I can tell she's sizing me up too, and it goes without saying that my Alice disguise, in the sorry shape that it's in, hasn't fooled her. With her, I'm Emily again, myself, and there's a small measure of comfort to be had in that.

Her arms dangle loosely at her sides. I see the knuckles on one hand twitch.

"You want to throw down again? You remember what happened the last time we fought in a bathroom," I say.

I'm not making a move at her, and she's standing there a couple of feet away. Even though I'm still a tad bigger than her and beat her last time, I don't have the energy in me for a fight to the death.

She chews her cheek, glaring at me. Clenching one fist, she points at me with her other hand.

"I should, do you know that? I should knock you out cold and feed you to the dogs!"

I'm nodding, my adrenaline kicking up already. Nothing would please me more than to dispel any illusions she might have about who's to blame and what should and shouldn't happen.

Hands on my damp hips, I shake my head at her.

"Because all this is my fault, right? Do you think I planned for any of this to happen? All I wanted was to hang out for drinks, but it ended up being this big weekend thing where one of us didn't make it back."

She shakes her head back at me, scowling. I'm starting to get the impression that her eyes are red not from tiredness but from emotion.

insane. If you'd only gone along with her, none of this would've happened," Taylor insists, and I purse my lips at her, eyes lowered.

"You're saying I should've handed my life over to her like you did, and that would've made it better? You know, Taylor, I thought maybe you'd recognize I did you a favor rejecting her ridiculous offer. Everything she was involved in was truly sick."

She eyes me warily.

"What are you talking about?"

Her face slackens, and I can see that she's listening. Taylor isn't a stupid girl, but she has the same hard background on the Dallas streets that I do. It makes me wonder how much she knew about what Alice was up to.

"I asked you both point-blank what was going on. All you fed me was some garbage about employee evaluations. My life was over, but that wasn't enough for Alice."

"What?" she asks.

"Don't give me that. You must've known something. Otherwise you wouldn't have been trying to stab me to death!"

She stamps her foot and grits her teeth in frustration. "That was only because you were going to ruin my life! I need this job and will do everything in my power to keep it," Taylor says, like she's voicing my thoughts from early in our trip.

"It looks like you made it to work today."

"And did you rat me out that I lied about my qualifications? I do actually have some skills," she says, though I don't know why she's trying to convince me. It's like she's threatening me with them, and I can see her ready to fight again with the wrong answer.

"No, I didn't tell anyone," I say, and she relaxes. I don't need to mention that Director Ron Zee couldn't care less and is probably ogling her explicit photos right now.

to try to hurt me."

And the way she says it sets me off. Not being hurt would've been nice when it was two versus one in the dark of that loft. But now I see that Taylor was Alice's pawn, also in the dark about her plans.

I'm scared about how much to tell her, because I trust her as much as I'd trust a dog to ignore red meat.

"Did you know?" I ask, deciding a point-blank question is the best way.

"Know what?"

Typical, I'll have to pry it out of her.

"Did you know the plan was for me to die all along?"

There, I said it, and Taylor gives me a hard look, not believing me either. I wouldn't believe it if I didn't hear it from the director's own mouth.

Taylor shakes her head.

"Things got out of hand. We were going to have fun. Alice wanted you as part of her group."

I cringe at describing Alice's idea of lifelong servitude as a social group, but we're beyond that. This is about what Alice did, what Director Ron Zee ordered her to do, and what Vice President Terry Glint ordered him to do. If it goes higher than that or has to do with the executive's wife, I'll find out.

"No, Taylor, Alice was instructed to make sure I didn't make it home alive. Someone in Bedrock wants me dead."

She backs away, her head shaking slightly.

"You're lying. I've heard you lie so many times you don't know what the truth even is."

I purse my lips and reach into my dry left pocket. I wave the check in front of her long enough for her to get a good look at it.

"This was given to me as soon as I walked in the door today

bonus check for taking out one Emily Marks."

Her eyes flit from the check to me, searching for a sign that I'm lying, and it crosses my mind that she might imagine I've forged a company check ahead of time to create support for my argument. I'm not that good, and she knows it.

A barely perceptible nod is the most assent I get from her that she understands I'm telling the truth.

"I've done some bad things, but never that. I'm...I'm sorry about the fight and trying to hurt you. I wasn't thinking clearly, but it wasn't the company."

I take a deep breath. "When the FBI came, Director Zee thought it was about the murder. He expected me to take the fall, admit guilt for my own death."

Unexpectedly, a wry smirk emerges on Taylor's face.

"You did your hair and pretended to be Alice. Your bodies are too different," she says.

I take a paper towel and try to wipe my bare arm and shoulder.

"I was wearing one of Alice's frumpy sweaters. No one out there knows I'm me. How did you make it back?"

It's a simple question, but it makes Taylor's eyes widen. She steps toward me, and I flinch, thinking she's jumping at me, but it's only to gently touch my arm.

"That part was crazy too. When I realized I was alone in the cabin," she says awkwardly, glossing over how I'd run and Alice had been stabbed to death, "I left immediately, knowing I had to get away."

That had to be shortly after I'd escaped, possibly while the guy from the bar was trying to choke the life out of me by the beach. If Taylor had been there, I imagine she might've helped him finish the job.

"How did you make it back?" I ask.

sighing.

A light goes on in my head.

"You met up with Wesley. I knew it," I say.

"No." Her ponytail flops around as she shakes her head. "It was the big local."

I gasp. "You mean Cletus?"

Emphatic nods follow. "Someone had attacked him, and he was staggering along the drive. I should've been running for my life, but I had nowhere to go and no way to get out of there, so I helped him to his car and even drove him back to his place with him vaguely giving directions while holding his head, bleeding badly."

"Oh my God, are you kidding me?" I'm in disbelief. "Wesley hit him after we discovered Mr. Chambers's body. Knocked him as hard as he could with the flashlight."

Her brown eyes widen.

"I got him home and put an ice pack against his head, but then I had to get out of there. I literally hitchhiked back to Dallas in the middle of the night. I was so sure that whoever picked me up was going to murder me, but I had no choice. It ended up being a trucker who didn't say a word to me the entire time."

Nodding, I take it all in, filling in a big gap of what happened, but I still don't know what happened to Wesley or the guy whose eye is out of commission.

"What about the sheriff's office? They haven't tried to reach you?"

She squinted. "Why would they?"

I gape at her, like the answer should be glaringly obvious.

"Because your hands were on the knife," I say, but she shrugs, not concerned at all.

"I've never been fingerprinted," she says.

detective or a forensic investigator.

"I told the sheriff and his deputy that the guy from the bar came in after us and got her," I say, more to myself than her. It seemed the neatest way to explain my injuries and the body without implicating myself.

Taylor appears taken aback, and I struggle to understand why until she opens her mouth.

"You protected me, even after everything I did."

Hmm, should I inflame her by saying I hoped and assumed she'd end up in jail for life now that she's standing right in front of me in an empty bathroom?

"You're right. I did," I say, nodding reluctantly.

People tell me it's OK to lie to protect other people's feelings, so it must be fine not to share the truth that I spent most of Sunday night thinking Taylor had been stabbed to death instead of Alice, and I was perfectly happy about it.

Suddenly, Taylor comes at me again, and this time she doesn't stop. I'm caught off guard and am even more surprised when her arms wrap around me, pulling me into a hug. I reluctantly touch her back, going through with the embrace even though I'm surely getting her a little wet.

When she releases a ragged breath, it suggests she really feels something and needs the sympathy. We've both been through a lot, and I always thought it was odd that we were at each other's throats.

Pulling back, she appears embarrassed about the embrace, and I muster a faint smile letting her know it was OK. On the streets of Dallas, even the girls are supposed to be hard, ruthlessly stepping on each other's necks to get what they want, which is usually some guy styling himself as a player who couldn't care about any of them.

Taylor says, rubbing one arm.

I give her a careful look, knowing full well I can only trust her as far as I can throw her, but I still need all the help I can get. If she wants to pitch in, there's no reason she can't start right now.

"I wouldn't be surprised if somebody here knows more. Shelley in particular has seemed close to Director Ron Zee from what I've seen today."

Taylor reaches back for the door and then glances back at me.

"I'm better off without her, Emily," she says. "By the way, did you get my note?"

My eyes widen, and I'm tempted to fish the little crumpled orange piece of paper out of my pocket.

"That was you?" I ask, relieved that I'm only finding out now. If I'd been thinking crazy Taylor was coming after me all day at work, that would've been too much. "How did you know where I was?"

She sets her hand on her hip and gives me a sly smirk.

"Someone told me my friend came to work looking like a train wreck. I went by your desk on the fourth floor, but there was this cute new guy there. That left only one other place you might be. I thought you might come find me."

I nod sheepishly, unable to tell her that I'd never figured it out, and right now I'm starting to think that was for the best. Earlier in the day, we might've been cutting each other to pieces.

"I was a little busy," I say, and Taylor raises an eyebrow.

"You still are."

She moves on out, and I follow her even though the beer has dried to my skin at this point.

But even though I'm still disgusting, it feels like a relief.

expected. We'll see how long it lasts.

I start to head out, my mind racing to churn through the turn of events and figure out what to do next. Right before I let go of the door, out of the corner of my eye I see one of the bathroom stall doors start to swing open.

A face appears for a fraction of a second. It's our server, Shaylene.

19

Despite the bathroom not smelling the best and my concern about being away from the table for so long, knowing that Shaylene listened in on my whole conversation with Taylor pulls me back into the bathroom faster than if I'd been shot with a harpoon.

I'm tempted to call Taylor so we can double team her, because we both have secrets we don't want to get out, but I'm hoping I can take care of this quickly and discreetly.

By the time I'm back inside, the stall door has mysteriously closed again. I wonder how much she heard, how much she figured out. She must know that license I gave her really is a fake, that I'm not Alice, possibly that we were involved in a murder and an assault. And that's only the beginning of what she could reasonably infer.

I glance underneath the door and can't see any feet. For all I know, she's standing on the toilet with her phone calling the police right now. She could be calling a coworker to help her get past me. If there are two things that won't help me right now, it's an encounter with the cops or being thrown out of Three Tequila Floor.

and scream and tell her bad things will happen if she doesn't come out now and keep her mouth shut. No, that won't work.

My second instinct is to ask nicely and beg her to forget what she heard so that I don't get in more trouble. It might work, but she'd probably want something for it. I could only imagine her asking for a four-digit tip or any number of things for her silence.

Thankfully I haven't said a word yet and can go with my third, best thought. Rather than saying anything to her at all, I go to the sink and turn on the faucet, making it seem like I've come in here to actually wash myself. I barely spritz my arm a little before shutting it off.

That's when the real waterworks start.

Sniffling and sighing loudly, I get my emotions up and let them get the best of me. It's not too hard, considering how much trouble I'm actually in, how I could've died and might still if I don't figure this out, how I have almost nothing to defend myself with, and how I even now have no idea why I'm such a big threat to the company.

Once I see my eyes start to water, I go to the side wall and slide down it, taking a seat on the gritty, smelly floor. I let loose with the sobs then, hands on my face, moaning intermittently.

I get so into it that I almost lose track of what's happening. What I thought was an Oscar-worthy performance starts to feel like real sadness. Why is this all happening to me? Why couldn't I have had a good family like we pretended in my picture for five seconds?

The stall door opens, but I don't stop crying, acting oblivious to what's around me. That's the trick. Shaylene could walk right on out the door and go back to work with plausible deniability that it wasn't her and that she never saw me.

But I'm betting she doesn't. She'll recognize me here with the room's harsh white light. I'm only five or so years older than her, and all of her sympathy hasn't been jaded out of her yet.

Mostly because she hasn't come across situations like this or people like me.

"Are you alright?" she asks hesitantly, perhaps feeling obligated because of her job.

"I'm fine. Go away," I say, shaking and looking at her with eyes that I know are anguished and red.

Shaylene's still here, standing near me, and I can guess she's trying to square my current state with everything she heard us talking about. Slowly, she kneels down in front of me, her bare knees on the tile in a way that can't be comfortable.

"What is it?" she asks.

I glance at her through my fingers and pretend to be surprised that it's her, the little red-haired snot who tried to make me guess the birthday on Alice's driver's license.

"It's nothing," I say and curl further into a ball.

But my crying stops, and I can hear her breathing, feel her eyes on me. Maybe it's a sordid interest in someone else's troubles or the novelty of another girl bawling on the floor in the restaurant bathroom, but she's well and truly hooked.

"If you'd only tell me—"

"It doesn't matter, not to you," I say slowly, but I'm watching her now while trying to judge how far to take playing hard to get. Every time I brush her off is a chance she'll take me up on it and leave. She lightly bites her lip and glances at the door. Thankfully nobody else has come in.

"I can call you a—"

"I'm in trouble," I gush before she takes this conversation in a direction I don't want it to go in. "I can't believe this is happening."

My knuckles are pressed to my lips, and the only sounds are

her cheeks but also some bruises on her arms. Whether they're from an accident here, a cat fight of her own, or courtesy of one of Dallas's fine gentlemen, I don't know.

"Is it someone from your work?" she asks, showing she heard plenty of what I was talking about.

My eyes widen, and I reach out hesitantly to her like I've seen a ghost.

"You shouldn't know about that. He'll come for you too."

"Who?" she asks quickly.

I glance at the door as if afraid someone might come in.

"I shouldn't be talking about this. Someone's been watching me. He's got a black windbreaker on. I can't go home, not now. He'll be watching the way I go home from work for a while."

She gives me a slow nod, and I trust that between this and what she's already heard that I've said enough.

"I am sorry about the spill and the thing with the license. I always do that with tables full of women. They usually think it's hilarious."

She takes my hand and helps me up, and we stand awkwardly together. I've got a couple of inches on her but am still acting unsteady. She's more naive and trusting than I thought. By the time I was eighteen, I'd been living on my own for more than a year during the trial and didn't trust anyone.

"Don't worry about it," I say.

Shaylene sighs and gives me a sidelong look.

"I should get back to work."

"Alright," I say, confident that she'll keep what she heard to herself. As she steps out of the bathroom, it crosses my mind that I'm the one being too trusting. Perhaps she'll call the cops the second she leaves the bathroom, even if she thinks she's doing it to protect me.

I stagger to the sink and look in the mirror, realizing I've got

face is puffy and red. I can't hide from the truth that the crying really wasn't fake.

One hand clutching the side of the sink, I look at my other opened palm in front of me and chide myself for my weakness. I may have developed a sour view of lying, but the truths I've learned from being on my own since age seventeen can't be forgotten for even a second.

I take my open palm and smack myself in the face as hard as I can, right on my bruise, which stings enough to feel like I'm igniting a fire on my face. Some moaning breaths follow as I recover and remind myself of the things I know deep in the bottom of my heart.

The only one I can ever count on is myself. I can't afford to be weak for even one minute. Giving up is not an option. Feeling sorry for myself is foolish and accomplishes nothing. I have to fight to make it through each and every day.

The bathroom door bursts open suddenly, startling me. It was only a matter of time until someone else came in.

But then I see that it's Shaylene again, leaning in with her arm propping the door open. I merely gape at her while she gives me a sympathetic look.

After swallowing, she says, "Before you arrived, the other girls at the table were talking about how they planned to stick you with the bill."

The door closes, and I again glance at the mirror. The teary squint in my eyes is gone. Only a hard glare remains.

20

I return to my table with my head held high and a confident stride, very used to taking my inner doubts and stuffing them down so deep that they can't see the surface.

The atmosphere is still enjoyable, and I think about ordering another drink, since the daiquiri is virtually gone, but I'm more hungry than thirsty and need to keep my head about me.

Shelley has gone somewhere, while the others are chatting about work. I subtly glance at Taylor, reflecting on how she was in on the plan to get me to cover everyone's drinks but didn't tell me. I don't know what it is that makes everyone think they can constantly take advantage of me, but they're about to learn it doesn't work that way.

Taylor notices me and brushes her hair back as she turns to me.

"Are you feeling better?" she asks, and I can't tell if she's being sarcastic.

"Nothing more refreshing than a beer bath," I say.

I notice Shelley returning from the side door with a grisly look on her face. Or maybe she's got a bit of a resting scowl face.

thirties. Fortunately, I probably won't live that long anyway.

"Uh oh," Janice says ominously as Shelley retakes her seat, shaking her head.

Shelley groans, and I feel a massive vent coming on.

"Do yourself a favor and never get married," she says, proceeding to finish off the rest of her beer, which has to be her third or fourth of the evening.

"Usually he doesn't bother to call," Gina says, and Shelley nods reluctantly.

"You're right about that. Usually it's a few days of passive aggression until I can deduce what he's in a snit about. But he knows we go out on Tuesday night and still is shocked when I'm not there with dinner prepared. I don't know how he hasn't starved to death being unable to cook for himself for one night."

There are sympathetic smirks around the table as everyone latches on to a new punching bag.

"What did you say?" Janice asks, and Shelley flashes a vicious grin.

"I told him to deal with it. When he started to say something, I told him that if I heard one more complaint, I wouldn't do his laundry. Then I told him that if I heard him whine, I wouldn't do the grocery shopping. It's all unbelievable. Silly me, I thought I'd have to get pregnant before I was responsible for taking care of a child."

It's easy enough for me to snicker along with the others, feeling like I got a taste of that with Wesley, who liked to jab me that I was bad at math but who couldn't make himself a peanut butter sandwich. But I'm distracted when I feel the sensation that someone is watching me.

Glancing over my shoulder, I try to see if somebody's behind me, but with so many people around I can't be sure. Straightening forward, I can't escape the feeling that someone is glaring

the bar.

There's no one obviously watching me, but I know myself enough to accept the creeping feeling that someone around is keeping a close eye on me. As much as I'd like to think I've attracted a fetching admirer among the patrons of Three Tequila Floor, considering how my day has been, I figure it's something far worse.

Someone has found out that I'm here.

I have to think the FBI agents or other cops would storm right in, but the man in the black windbreaker who grabbed me is another story. I couldn't even see who he was, and there was so much noise that I could hardly hear his voice, but someone like that would be able to watch me from the other side of the restaurant or through the windows.

It makes me feel unsettled, unsafe.

Escaping a murder plot at work only to die at the hands of a random creeper from Hochatown would be so disappointing.

Sure I can feel someone's eyes on me again, I shift suddenly to catch them and see a figure striding in my direction from behind. Sulking, I recognize that it's only Shaylene, who is back with a glowing smile.

"Is there anything else I can get y'all?" she asks, taking her usual spot between Taylor and I.

I shake my head, definitely not about to have another drink when there's a possibility that someone out to get me is hanging around. Maybe my confession to Shaylene was a little too close to the truth.

"It's about time for me to get going anyway," Janice says. "My cats don't have to call me up to demand dinner."

The others appear to be finished as well, but then Shelley pipes up, "I'll have one last summer, but you can go ahead and bring the check."

away.

I sit back and try to relax, which isn't easy considering it won't be long until everyone leaves and I'm left alone again to deal with whoever is lurking about. But I at least act casual while waiting for one of them to do the inevitable.

Shelley, who's already had twice as much to drink as anyone, leans my way and then blinks as if she's only now noticing something.

"Your cheeks are looking pink," she says, and I smile.

"Yeah, one is enough for me to start to feel it."

She glances around for confirmation before again settling her eyes back on me.

"So, we do have this thing where the newcomers pick up the tab and then we take turns treating each other. You don't mind, do you? It shouldn't be that much," she says sweetly, as if she hadn't been ordering drink after drink, confident that someone else would pay for it.

Thanks to the heads-up from Shaylene, I had plenty of time to prepare. The thought crossed my mind to act like I'd forgotten my card at work, pretending like I would've been more than willing otherwise. It's not even my money, so who cares, right?

But then I think about how Shelley hazed me on my first day of work and how the entire HR staff trash-talked me on the Slack channel before foisting me on to the FBI. Now they want me to cover their after-work drinks. I want to take my black socks and shove them down her throat.

I blink, acting surprised. Everyone is watching me, including Taylor, who doesn't appear bothered that I might need to cover a couple of her drinks despite knowing I'm the first name on the company's kill list.

"Oh, the server told me that since she gave me a beer shower that my drink is on the house, so technically I didn't order

there will never be a next time.

Shelley's eyebrows twitch as she narrows her eyes at me. So much for being flexible and dealing with a different answer than she expected. I see her digging in from here, but it's actually Janice beside me who speaks up.

"That makes it even easier though. You still get to pay less, and then next time someone else will get it, even if you don't get doused," she says. It sounds friendly enough, but I can see she's forcing her smile. The way she's clutching the armrest of her chair is a dead giveaway.

Maybe if Bedrock was a better place to work, these ladies wouldn't be ready to slit each other's throats over a hundred-dollar bar tab, but that doesn't mean I'm going to cave to them.

I give Janice the most sympathetic look I can, hands gripping each other tight between my legs and shrugging.

"But if I didn't actually get anything, why would I have to pay at all? Besides, don't you think it would be better to let me know as soon as I got here that I was going to be expected to fork over for everything?"

Janice's smile drops, and she shakes her head almost imperceptibly. It's doubtful that she even listened to anything I was saying after she got the gist that I wasn't about to give her a free ride. Taylor rolls her eyes, and the other two women look like I've sucked all of the oxygen out of the room.

Shelley, probably half-drunk, has her head in one hand and is glaring at me.

"Alice, we all paid when it was our turn, and now it's yours. Time to be a big girl and suck it up."

She waves the back of her fingers at me, like she's scooting me along, as if that would make me compliant, but little does she know that I eat insults like that for breakfast. Bars like this aren't my element because I can socialize with coworkers. No, I

on my mind.

I wonder if Shelley can see the gleam in my eye.

"Deal with it like you're dealing with your leeching husband? It kind of feels like you come here and get as drunk as you can to numb yourself from having to deal with him when you get home."

Her mouth opens as she fixates on me, her mind blown. The snarl comes next, gritted teeth.

"At least I have a husband. I can't remember the last time I saw you with a man," she said.

I burst out laughing. That line might've worked on Alice, but this is not an area I have trouble with. And she's got to be fully drunk even to go there.

"Wait a second. Are you seriously trying to criticize me because I'm not married yet? I'm not even twenty-four years old! You think there aren't a dozen guys in here I couldn't walk out with if I wanted to? Look, Shelley, I'm sorry you had to settle for a lazy louse that you need to do everything for in order to keep around, but don't take it out on me. Let me guess that you don't only drink on Tuesday evenings either. What, five, six, seven times a week?"

There are some gasps around the table, and Shelley's face has turned a shade of red that almost matches my strawberry daiquiri.

"You don't even know. I've forgotten what it's like to be young and stupid," she says, about to blow her top.

"Or one of those," I mutter quickly.

Taylor has to clamp her lips down to avoid laughing.

Both Shelley and I open wide to commence with an epic squabble, but Janice raises a hand and leans in between us. I give her a raised eyebrow to ask if she really wants to get in the

free drinks.

"Hey, that's enough. Let's calm down for a minute. I think we're missing something important. Treating each other is how we all show some company spirit, Alice," she says, giving me a look and craning her neck as if to say that alone should easily settle the matter.

There's that name again. Alice. I can't stand it and should've known when I took it that I wouldn't be able to tolerate posing as her for even one full day. And how long has she sat next to Alice without really noticing what she looks like?

"Company spirit?" I ask calmly, hiding how that sets me off more than the suggestion I'm inadequate with the opposite sex.

"Yeah," Janice says, happily brushing her brown curls behind her ear, "working at Bedrock is more than a job. It's about building community and empowering each other."

I nod attentively, waiting for her to finish so I can dump some cold water on this.

"Building community and empowering each other, yes, like on the Slack channel, right?"

"What?" Janice asks, squinting. Then it hits her, and she casts a sidelong look at Shelley.

"The Slack channel," I say, making eye contact with the three women here who aren't from the department. "I'm not sure if everyone knows most of what's done in HR all day is gossiping on Slack about coworkers, laughing at their problems, cruelly belittling people based on their appearances, and coming up with ways to torment them."

Shelley eyes the other women, scoffing for their benefit.

"That is not what's going on at all. I can't believe you would say something like that," she insists.

I tap my chin.

"You can't believe I would say that, but you would believe

department a nervous breakdown. If I'm not mistaken, there's a thread on every single other employee, or almost all of them, going into their personal problems, ridiculing them, and discussing how to exploit their misfortunes," I say.

"That's a gross mischaracterization. We're trying to help people," Janice says, huffing and tossing a napkin on the table, but I can see she's feeling the heat and looking at me in a way that says what I'm doing is unforgivable.

Good, because I'll never forgive them.

"How does it help people to promise them raises they'll never get?" I ask.

Gina pipes up from the end of the table. "Is this for real?" she squeaks awkwardly.

Shelley ignores her.

"You're a liar and a brown-nosing loser who'll do anything Director Zee says," Shelley shoots back.

Even trying to kill me. Sounds about right for Alice. Too bad I'm not her.

"If I'm lying, why not show them the channel? Give them two minutes," I say with relish.

Both Shelley and Janice freeze until the dam bursts.

"Utter nonsense!"

"You can't believe a word that comes out of her mouth!"

The rest of us sit back and watch as they get overly defensive about something that they know is undeniable. Maybe they can act like it's under control now, but as soon as the others walk into work in the morning, there's no way everyone doesn't get in an uproar about it.

Shelley is in the middle of a rant about Bedrock's ethical code when Taylor manages to interrupt them with a voice softer and more innocent than anything I've ever heard from her before.

Shelley freezes and glances over at the girl with the ponytail and the Cowboys jersey, who is sitting back and tracing a finger around her ear.

It takes her five seconds to spit out, "No!"

Taylor's eyebrows drop, not buying the obvious lie. She puts both hands on the table and leans forward from her side.

"Unbelievable. What do you say about me, huh?" She has to keep going when they don't respond. "Tell me. I'm going to find out."

Shelley and Janice are stewing but have no way out and refuse to answer, leaving me to reach out and set my hand on Taylor's.

Speaking gently as well and looking her square in the eyes, I say, "They know about the pictures. They laugh about them every single day."

Taylor looks like she's ready to breathe fire, but instead Shelley bursts out of her seat to stand over the table, pointing a finger right at me.

"You're one to talk, Alice! You're the worst one in the office. All you ever do is sit on the Slack channel and bad mouth anyone you happened to see that day. I always thought it was vile and disgusting."

I rise slowly from my seat to stand eye to eye with her from across the table. No doubt what she's saying is true, but there's a key piece of information she's missing. I go ahead and brush my hair back as far as I can with it at this length. Hair in my eyes hiding my face really isn't my thing.

"That's a good point, or it would be," I say, building up steam. "Except I'm not Alice Patterson. I'm Emily Marks! Now who's clueless and pathetic? I'm out of here. Have a good time in the office tomorrow."

Everyone is stunned, and I gloat shamelessly as I turn

more I have to say, and I can walk away confident that this is the last girls' night they'll ever have.

One loose end remains. I did of course lie about my drink being free and need to pay before I get out of Three Tequila Floor and figure out what to do next.

Fortunately, I notice a familiar sight as I start to weave in between some standing patrons and nearby tables. Shaylene is coming my way with what appears to be Shelley's drink. I go ahead and fish a ten out and hand it to her for my drink.

Her eyes fix on me, and she doesn't seem to notice that she's taken the money and tucked it into her pouch. Instead, I get this concerned look from her, and she leans in close.

"Don't look now, but this guy at the front entrance has been watching you."

Suddenly stricken and completely ignoring her advice, I immediately jerk up and look over upon hearing that my phantom feeling of being watched has been validated.

I fully expect to see someone with an eye patch and a black windbreaker, but instead the last person I would've guessed is standing close to the bar, casually checking me out as he leans against a beam.

Our eyes catch. I don't know what this means, but my heart skips a beat.

It's Miles.

21

Considering I went through the entire previous conversation at the table feeling perfectly calm, the bundle of nerves that pops up suddenly upon spotting Miles across the barroom floor leaves me confused.

I stroll over to him without any particular rush, giving me a moment to try to figure out what's going on in my head and my body. He looks super cute in his shirt and tie, hair still a mess and teeth sparkling white, contrasting with his light tan, but I don't get flustered no matter how hot someone is. No, it's something else that's stirring these feelings.

The surprise after figuring I'd never see him again is helping his cause, as is how he patiently waits for me to come to him. I find myself entirely willing to put in the work closing the distance, while so many times I would've said a guy who can't bother to walk across a room to get to me is out of luck.

Even though there's plenty of eye contact, he's got a serious expression with brows furrowed that's telling me he's not here by accident or for fun. When I'm a few steps away, that's when he makes his move, setting a hand on my shoulder and nudging me closer.

"Miles, what are you doing here?" I ask at almost the same time.

He leans in, glancing over my shoulder and around us. He's probably doing the exact same thing I did when I first walked in, checking for other coworkers from Bedrock.

"You said you were going out after work. I checked three other bars before coming here," he says.

Suddenly, his eyes widen, and he leans back right when he was about to get to the important part.

"But why?" I ask, but he's fully distracted now by something behind me.

"So who's this?" calls a feminine voice from behind me.

I spin around to find that Taylor didn't take long to follow me over from the table, and I grow apprehensive that I'll have trouble finding out what Miles wants while she's around. Still, Taylor did back me up somewhat with the other women, so I do the normal thing and answer her question.

"This is Miles. He's Emily Marks's replacement," I explain, cueing her in. It looks like I'm not completely rid of being Alice yet, especially not when Miles would be horrified at everything about me.

Taylor walks right up to us, except she's ignoring me like I'm not even here. She reaches out limply so Miles can shake her hand. An uncomfortable feeling in my stomach grows.

"Hi, Miles. I'm Taylor, but I also go by MathSlut12," she says.

I bite my tongue. Yeah, Taylor has some personal boundary issues and comes off overeager. And from the looks of it, her romp with Wesley over the weekend didn't leave her satisfied for long.

And the way she's looking him over, how she's facing him directly, and how she's shifted her weight onto one foot, she's

He's so great, and she would crush his innocence.

"It's nice to meet you," he says simply.

I have to think fast to come up with a way to save him.

"He's my boyfriend," I say with a self-indulgent grin, drawing surprised looks from both of them. This is perfect and will leave Taylor with no choice but to keep herself in check or risk incurring my wrath.

Miles squints at me.

"No, I'm not," he says plainly.

My inner grumbles start. He should know if a girl wants to pretend to be his girlfriend that he should play along. Curse the handful of girls who exist in Upstate New York who didn't teach him this.

I laugh and roll my eyes, bumping him in the hips to try to give him the message.

"Yes, you are," I say.

He shakes his head.

"But I'm not though."

"Stop that," I say, laughing hollowly and really wanting to strangle him. "We don't have to hide it."

Taylor narrows her eyes, watching us carefully.

"What are you talking about?" Miles asks.

I glance at him, widening my eyes in a flash. *Come on!* But all I can do is keep laughing and acting like we're together.

"He's such a joker," I say, turning my attention to Taylor. "Don't you love a guy who can make you laugh?"

"I don't get it. We're not dating," he says.

I stifle a sigh and grit my teeth. Hints of that word I can't remember come to mind again. Somebody who keeps saying things that are true, he's this type of person. Ahh, maybe one day I'll think of it.

and exert my will over both of them.

Still laughing, I fully tip over in his direction, practically making him catch me. It's a good thing he doesn't let me drop to the floor, but it gets his arms around me and gives me a chance to drape one of mine over his shoulders.

"Oh, this guy, no one will accuse him of being a stage-five clinger!" I say, winking at Taylor.

"Alright," Taylor says, crossing her arms.

It looks like she's at least seen that I've claimed him as mine, even though it took practically rubbing myself on him to do it. I couldn't allow his precious heart to be broken by Taylor and her lies and scams and knives.

Besides, I liked him from the moment I saw him...this morning when I was busy pretending to be someone else and faking an employee onboarding session.

Miles lets me go and shrugs at me, which I suppose is the best I'll be able to get out of him right now without it being written in a signed contract.

"The reason I was trying to find you though is because what you said earlier at lunch made me think of something," he says, catching my interest. "What if Bedrock does have something shady going on with it?"

I'm nodding feverishly, but before I can get anything out, Taylor speaks up.

"We were talking about that a few minutes ago. There's something seriously messed up going on, and we're trying to get to the bottom of it."

I flinch out of surprise. What Taylor said was actually helpful, and I couldn't have put it better myself. I start to wonder if some of Alice's influence is starting to fade from her. Taylor is of course referring to the executives who want me dead, but she wisely didn't spell it all out and step on Miles's toes.

"Exactly, so I spent a lot of the afternoon trying to dig as deeply into the financials as I can, looking for any kind of impropriety. Specifically, I've been trying to get some of the core metrics related to the Q Fund."

Taylor gawks at him.

"You think there's something fishy going on with the Q Fund? That's the company's bread and butter. Everyone knows that," she says.

Miles sighs and crosses his arms in deep thought. "It's no wonder why. Consistent growth year after year, always beating the market index funds, an inexhaustible demand for shares." He scratches his nicely cut jaw. "But what if it's too good to be true?"

I gasp at the implication, even though this conversation is taking on a distinctly nerdy vibe that is leaving me behind.

"So you think it is too good to be true?" I ask, repeating him.

He shakes his head and strains, and I can almost see his brain working.

"I can't say that, because there's no evidence. And that's a big part of the problem. The amount of documentation related to the Q Fund is extremely minimal. Without more information, it's impossible to make an informed judgment."

I nod. I'm not sure which is worse, potentially defrauding hundreds of thousands of customers or trying to give me a flat line on a heart rate monitor. I mean, I know which is worse for me. That would be dying because of a company hit job. But messing with a lot of people's money is bad too.

"What do you think it could be?" Taylor asks. Maybe it's only because Miles has unconsciously suckered her in with his looks, but it seems like she cares about this.

Miles hems and haws. "Your guess is as good as mine. They could be cherry-picking data for investors, cooking the books a

sured sales tactics."

I exchange glances with Taylor, who like me recognizes technical terms for legal scams, but I'm not sure how it could be a rip-off with everyone making so much money. Most of what I get is that Miles will make a much better financial planner than I ever would.

"Do you think this is why the FBI showed up today?" Taylor asks Miles, but I quickly speak up to show that I'm not totally useless in this conversation.

"They said they were looking into an unauthorized transaction, but nobody mentioned the Q Fund," I say, catching a look from Miles. That was news to him.

"There was an unauthorized transaction that got the FBI's attention?" He seems skeptical. I have to admit it sounds weird.

"Nobody was able to find even the faintest trace of anything out of place. We looked through everything," Taylor says.

The questions get me thinking though. Possible shenanigans with the Q Fund, an unauthorized transaction, and people at the company wanting me dead. How did it all add up? Were all of these things connected?

Because Miles doesn't know what is happening to me, bringing it up now isn't a good idea. I don't think he'll ever be ready to step into my dark world.

"When I heard that executive, Vice President Terry Glint, talking with an agent, he was very concerned about something ruining their upcoming plans," I say.

Miles watches me to see if I'll say more, but he doesn't need to know that the thing the company is worrying about is me. Slowly, he shakes his head.

"If I'd been on the job more than one day, maybe I would've heard about that guy, but right now I'll be happy if I can find a way to access more information about the Q Fund."

fists.

"I was actually about to go get my laptop to look him up, and I bet if you had access to the accounting department's data, it could help you piece together more about the Q Fund," she says. "The laptop's right in my car. If only we'd driven separately to Hochatown!"

I laugh weakly, but Miles is intrigued.

"That would be great," he says.

"It's a few minutes to my car and back, but I'm going," Taylor says, starting off.

Miles blinks, seemingly dazed at everything we've stumbled upon, and he doesn't even know the half of it. I'm stunned too and wonder if I might actually find out why the company wants me dead.

Are they afraid I'll somehow ruin a monster investment fund worth probably a billion dollars? The idea seems ridiculous.

But what makes much more sense are the two open seats at the bar, so I tug Miles closer and point.

"Might as well," I say, happy at the prospect of having some time with him. And I'd better make the most of it before Taylor manages to steal some of his attention with her numbers talk.

"Absolutely," he says, smiling at me, and I like everything about that.

We slide onto the stools and settle in under the bright lights with the liquor bottles in front of us and drinkers carousing on each side. It feels warm and lively, the way I'd imagined it would be since I first showed up, and having Miles here makes it even better.

I hope Shelley saw me with him on her way out.

Now that it's only me and Miles, I go ahead and take my advice and sit back, thinking and feeling a lot of things but not saying a word. We make brief eye contact a couple of times, and

some kind of social issue and needs me to write an instruction manual for him.

"Can I buy you a drink?"

There we go!

I grin at him, psyching myself up and wishing I could live in this moment forever, but I'm going to have to throw him a curveball.

"Normally I would say yes, but I did just finish one, and actually I'm really starving."

He gives me a knowing look and then flags down the bartender, a big guy with hairy arms who's sweating more than the chilled beer bottles.

"Hey, excuse me, can we get a plate of nachos here?" he asks before turning to me. "Is that alright with you?"

"You read my mind," I say, my mouth already watering.

Miles orders a beer for himself and then turns to me, elbow perched on the edge of the bar.

"There's something else you mentioned earlier at our lunch date that has been on my mind as well," he says while I look him over.

I get lost in his dark eyes and messy hair, my thoughts drifting. Is this our second date in one day? Sounds serious.

"Oh yeah, and what's that?" I ask coyly. He should know I love talking about things I've said.

He takes a deep breath and looks me in the eyes.

"You said everything I know about you is wrong."

Oh boy. The discomfort comes in quickly, and I start to squirm, wanting to innocently enjoy this for a few more moments before something about me comes up that scares the daylights out of him. But he insists on heading right for it.

Crossing my arms over my stomach, I shift away, looking for

thought I'd see the day when I wanted her to save me.

But as I look out over the bar, I see something else. On the stool, I can see over many of the tables to the set of windows by the side door.

There's a distinct shape there of someone peering in through the glass. The glare from the lights prevents me from making out his face, but the shine on the black windbreaker practically gives me a heart attack.

Miles isn't the only one who managed to find me.

The creep stalking me is here too.

22

The nachos come, and I try to focus on the tortilla chips covered in melted cheese, guacamole, and sour cream. There are little sliced jalapeño bits sprinkled on top as well. It's much more appealing than thinking about the guy outside who followed me across state lines and grabbed me in the entryway lobby to the Bedrock building.

The pile of nachos even slightly beats out looking at Miles, who has his eyes on me like he wants to visually perform an X-ray scan of my soul. That feeling comes over me again that I got when I first saw him, and it becomes a little clearer.

There are so many parts of myself and my life that I don't like, and he deserves better than for me to hide things from him.

"Yum," I say lamely, chomping on another chip and hoping the conversation will go anywhere else other than what's on his mind.

Instead, he keeps subtly appraising me, and I imagine what he must be thinking. How can you sit there like that and act like everything is fine when your whole life is a dumpster fire? If he said that out loud, I'd probably die on the spot, because I don't have a good answer.

His voice is gentle, playful even, but it's tearing me to pieces.

"Yes," I say, wishing I couldn't. It was a nice lunch, but now I'm wishing I'd hidden myself more. This is worse than crying in the bathroom. If I bury every last piece of myself so deep, no one can ever use them to hurt me.

He scoots a little closer and grins. I'm glad he thinks this is fun. That makes one of us.

"You said everything I know about you is false," he says, raising an eyebrow, but I don't take the bait. "So I've been trying to think about what that means."

I give him a sidelong look, wary.

"And what did you come up with?"

He glances at me and nods as if he's got me pinned.

"Simple. You color your hair or wear lifts in your shoes or embellish a little when talking about yourself. It's not a big deal."

The laughter is painful as it escapes me. I snort and shake my head at him. It's bittersweet to think those could be the things that are wrong with me and that he's naive enough to think that might be it.

My gut instinct is to lie. Or perhaps it wouldn't even be a lie. My hair is slightly colored to look more like Alice's. I could say yes and put the issue to rest, but I can't.

"That's not even close," I say, back to faking tranquility while my insides are twisted in a knot.

"Then what is it?" he asks, looking at me with his head slightly lowered, his eyes smoldering.

I can't tell him that either, as much as it breaks me to admit. I'm trapped.

Somber, I say, "You don't want to know, Miles. Look, you're a nice guy. Let's eat and have a drink and then part ways, never to see each other again. Forget about everything I said or looking

involved in."

I say it for his benefit, but he pulls back, looking hurt for a moment, and that stings me worse than anything. I'm already causing him pain, which is all I seem to be good at. Even when I'm trying to be nice, my tongue is sharper than it should be.

His smile has dropped, and he looks at me plainly. He should already be running for the hills, but he's not, and I don't know why.

"Tell me one thing that's true," he says, and I immediately start shaking my head. "One thing, Alice."

That name again grates against me. It's like she's here, haunting me from beyond the grave. I was too afraid to tell her and Taylor the truth from the beginning, and look where it got me.

I slowly reach into my pocket and pull out the picture in the little frame, the one of my family that I got from my desk, which is now Miles's. I hold it in front of me and show it to him, this snapshot I treasure of a family that wasn't like this for more than a manufactured second.

Diedre and Martin Marks were on the drab, fraying sofa we had in our cramped apartment while my sister and I sat in their laps. Melanie waved a TV remote while I gazed at it in amazement, our parents laughing behind us. We couldn't have been ten. Picture perfect and totally fake, but the memories aren't all bad.

Miles leans in to take a closer look at the picture.

"There was one summer when my mom had this brilliant idea for my sister and I to run a lemonade stand in our neighborhood. Melanie and I had so much fun talking to people that we didn't even care when Mom took all the money and said we'd do it again in another neighborhood the next day. We spent the whole summer all over town selling lemonade, except

still so nice even though by the end, after we'd probably made Mom thousands of dollars, we were basically selling cups of water."

Miles couldn't hide his cringe, and I couldn't blame him. The memory makes me sick to think about, but at the same time it's the best one I have. Better than the times my sister and I went to bed hungry or when my parents would argue or play tricks on us. The tricks turned into worse as we got older, and then there was the car accident. After that, things really went off the rails.

"That really happened?" he asks.

I nod, and for some reason he brightens up.

"There, that wasn't so bad, was it? Now I know one true thing about you. What else?"

I shift uncomfortably, wishing we could go back to idle flirting. The thought hits me to get up and run as I've done so many times before, but that feeling that I'm being watched sticks with me. I have nowhere to go.

"Miles, please..."

He sets his hand on mine suddenly, and I freeze up. It jolts me awake in a way that I don't expect. I should've taken him up on that offer for another drink.

"Let it all go," he says, looking into my eyes. "Whatever it is you think isn't enough or isn't what you wanted, somehow it got you here. You don't have to be anything other than what you are."

I give him a wary look, seriously doubting that he has much of an idea where here is for me or who I am. But he's listening and wants to know, and I get that feeling again, and this time it's crystal clear. I know what it is about Miles that I like, and it isn't his cute nose or dark-brown eyes.

He makes me want to be a better person.

Swallowing, I don't know where to begin. I'm used to lying

are all gummed up.

"I'm not Alice," I admit.

"Yeah," he says, and when he says it, I'm more shocked than he is.

"You knew?"

He glances at the picture, and I put it away, feeling foolish that I didn't think he would've recognized it.

"You're Emily."

I nod reluctantly, like being myself is a hard thing to admit to.

"Yeah."

"It's the company's fault that you don't have your job anymore and that you've been pretending to be Alice."

I nod more emphatically. He purses his lips and peers at me closely, like he can read more on my bruised face.

"Because you're here and she's not, something happened to her, and this is why you're so bitter about Bedrock."

In a way, I'm relieved at how much easier it is to simply agree rather than explain it all myself. He must've gone to a good college to figure all of this out so quickly. It feels like he gets me.

"Yes, and it's the most terrible, maddening, dangerous situation I've ever been in," I say, and it feels good to actually vent about it as myself to someone who's on my side.

Miles's ability to listen without judgment is incredible, like he's one of those counselors that I hear some people talk about their problems with. When he's formulating a response, I start to worry that he's going to get into the gory details. I nervously stuff another chip in my mouth.

"But why do you think all this is happening?" he asks, and even that simple question is a weight off my shoulders. I'd rather not have to incriminate myself in this bar with so many people around.

was going on today, I overheard the agents talking to a vice president I believe is Terry Glint. He was very concerned that I might pose a problem to something they have going on. I would ruin it, in his exact words, and he and his wife are furious. It makes no sense. I don't even know these people and had only worked at the company for a few weeks."

Miles leans back, taking it all in, and it makes me regret saddling him with my burden. He's starting a new job and doesn't need to be dipping his toe into an attempt to wipe out an entry-level worker he moved across the country to replace.

There's some movement out of the corner of my eye, and we both shift to see Taylor sweeping back into the bar, laptop in hand.

Before she can get here, Miles sets his hand on my knee, making me jerk my head back to him. His lightly tanned face is so handsome and so serious.

"I want to figure out what's going on," he says.

I forget to breathe for a moment until Taylor shows up, a little winded but with a big smile on her face.

"OK, Miles, Alice, I'm back and ready," she says, and I hold up my hand at her.

"You can forget the Alice stuff. He knows," I say, and Taylor gives me a suspicious look.

"You told him who you are? Wait, he didn't try to make you pay for a drink, did he?" Taylor asks.

"Ha ha, very funny," I say sarcastically, even though it actually is hilarious, and I probably would've laughed if it wouldn't make her look good in front of Miles. "But he knows that something happened and that the Bedrock upper management seems to have a personal interest in me."

I start to wonder what we can figure out once we put our

there are only two seats here and three of us.

Taylor goes up to the burly guy with the beard seated next to Miles and taps him on the shoulder.

"Excuse me, you're in my seat," she says, hand on her hip and head cocked.

He squints at her.

"I've been here for thirty minutes," he says.

"I was sitting right here until I just went to the bathroom," she says.

The only thing better than watching Taylor grind the poor guy down until she can steal his seat is the realization that I'll never have to pretend to be Alice again. The relief comes with a wellspring of optimism that we'll finally be able to put the past to rest and figure out what's going on.

That's when my phone rings, or rather Alice's phone. I dig it out and see that the number is calling from Idabel, Oklahoma, and I get a sinking feeling in my gut when I realize that Idabel is one of the towns I passed on the way back from Hochatown.

Reluctantly, I answer and say hello.

"Is this Alice Patterson?" the voice on the other side says, though I have to strain to hear it over the bar's noise.

I nearly choke when I answer, "Yes," but then the noise drowns out anything coming over the speaker, even though it's jammed into my ear. "Sorry, but I didn't catch that."

I start to think about where the noise won't be so loud and shift out of my seat when the caller tries again.

"This is the McCurtain County Sheriff's Office calling about the incident this past weekend. We need to talk."

23

Dismayed, I stare blankly at the phone in my hand like it's a dead fish.

The sheriff's office from Hochatown is calling? This is the absolute last thing I need, but it shouldn't be all that surprising either. It hasn't even been forty-eight hours since I served the sheriff and his deputy a big lie salad, and I'm lucky that it held out this long.

"Hold on a second until I can get to someplace quieter," I say, but really my mind is racing, and I'm stalling to think of what I can say to keep them off my back.

How did they poke a hole in my story that my identity is that of the victim, that the victim is me, and that the killer is another guy who wasn't technically involved in that at all, when actually I did it? What could've gone wrong? How about everything?

I glance over my shoulder at Taylor flipping open her laptop while shoulder to shoulder with Miles. That's a disaster waiting to happen, and I still can't believe Taylor is actually trying to help. Either her knife-wielding was just the result of a psychotic moment when she thought she was going to lose her job, or maybe she's only doing it to try to steal Miles from me.

leaving me no choice but to quickly find a place to talk. That means going outside, which is the absolute last place I want to go.

I weave around some standing patrons, ducking a little in the vain hope that the guy stalking me won't notice that I'm on the move. Instead of going to the shady side door, I go for the open main entrance with the bright lights and the bouncer.

It seems like there's a smaller chance of being kidnapped or killed out there. Not zero chance, but a smaller one. The prospect of running into the guy from the Hochatown bar whose eye I drilled through using an ancient Native American arrowhead after he tried to choke me to death helps me feel better about blaming him for Alice's death.

I step through the entrance and give a tepid smile to the jacked bouncer so that he'll recognize me when he needs to give the police sketch artist a description after my imminent disappearance. It's been fully dark for a while now, and a breeze has kicked up that gives the skin on my face a chilly nip.

Only now that I'm outside do I realize how hot it was inside the bar and how worked up I'd gotten over the server, Shelley, and Miles.

When I step close to the curb, I put the phone to my ear, hoping that the sheriff gave up on me and ended the call. No such luck. How come a sheriff is working into the evening like this, anyway?

"Hello?" I say again, and the sheriff starts right up.

"Hi, Alice, I'm calling to follow up after the incident in Hochatown this past Labor Day weekend. Let me start by asking about your injuries," the gruff sheriff says, stopping without actually asking.

"I'm recovering," I say, which is putting it lightly. There are some other people around outside the bar, and cars are cruising

thing at once.

"Is there anything else you'd like to tell us that might be helpful for our investigation?" he says.

There's an edge he can't keep out of his voice, tipping me off that the question is a trap. He must know something, and this may be my chance to come clean with reduced consequences, but more likely he's hoping I'll divulge something useful so he can make a quick arrest and be done with it. I'm not any more inclined to go to jail than I was Monday morning when I regained consciousness by the lake.

This feels like the opposite of my FBI interrogation. Instead of knowing nothing, I know everything, but Mom's advice is still gold. Keep my mouth shut as much as possible.

"No," I say, not even asking if they'd found the guy who killed Alice and Jim Chambers. What's the point of asking when he's lurking around the building, probably not twenty feet away from me?

"We've been reviewing the evidence and comparing it to your statement," he says, pausing long enough for me to grit my teeth as a bout of nervousness takes over. "There appear to be some discrepancies."

The cooler air is starting to get to me, as is this phone call that threatens to upend my life for decades. Now that Taylor's being so helpful, maybe she wouldn't mind taking responsibility for this murder. I'm tempted to get the sheriff's office her fingerprints from a glass to help them figure out who was holding the knife.

"Oh," I say as ambiguously as possible, not completely monotone but not transparently guilty either.

I hold my elbow against my chest. My shirt is still slightly damp from the spilled beer, and there is not a lot of fabric to this undershirt to keep me warm. Throwing away Alice's hideous

All that dust would've helped me retain more body heat.

"We're going to need you to come down to the station to talk some things through," he says, which also sounds like a trap.

I can easily see talking some things through leading to handcuffs and a short walk to a holding cell before being transferred to the county jail. I have serious doubts that Oklahoma jails are nice places.

Can I just say no thanks and hang up?

"It's kind of late, and I'm not in the area anymore," I say.

"We can refer this to your local police department or sheriff's office," he says, quickly cutting through my flimsy excuse.

I close my eyes, succumbing to the realization that dealing with this sheriff's office and one young woman's grisly stabbing in a hot tub might get in the way of me trying to find out why she was trying to kill me in the first place.

"I can check my schedule and give you a call soon about when I can make it back to talk to you," I say.

"Tomorrow," he says loudly enough that I could've heard it clearly even inside the bar. "You'll call tomorrow and plan to come as quickly as you can."

I sigh. We seem to have different definitions of the word "soon" and "quickly," and that's going to pose a problem for me.

"Sure," I say.

After a perfunctory goodbye, the call ends, and I glare at Alice's phone like it bitterly betrayed me. My phone never would've done such a thing to me, but it's in tiny pieces in Hochatown.

I glance around, from the entrance of Three Tequila Floor to the curb to down the sidewalks, until my eyes land on the perfect solution to my problem in a narrow alley right beside the bar.

A dumpster is waiting there, wide open and accessible. I'm

to take a few steps forward before I can pitch the phone under-hand into the trash receptacle's beckoning maw. A nice loud *thunk* echoes when it hits the bottom.

With one swift motion, I've wiped out the last trace of Alice and a pestering murder investigation simultaneously. Brilliant. And I never left myself open to being accosted by a deranged stalker to boot.

Now to return to Miles and Taylor to see what they're finding out about Bedrock's Q Fund and plot about my death.

I turn around to head back into the bar but step right into a black windbreaker, a large body with it completely blocking my path.

I flail frantically, trying to get some distance, but the guy puts his hands up.

"Whoa, whoa, whoa," he says, and I look up, making out his face against the glare of the streetlight.

It's Wesley.

Are you kidding me?

Then *I* attack *him*.

24

I jump onto Wesley, wrapping my legs around his waist and holding on with one hand so I can club him on the shoulder with my other fist.

He staggers back but stays upright with me on him, and all I want to do is tear his face off. Those blue eyes and short blond hair are the last things I want to see right now, but after a couple of shots at him, I give up on whacking him with my fist and start clutching that windbreaker by the chest and yanking on it.

"What is wrong with you?" I shout into his face. "Why can't you walk up and say hi to me like a normal person? Instead you stalk me all day. I thought you were the maniac from the lake!"

There's a sickening taste in my mouth from all the times I caught glimpses of him. What about the time he grabbed me from behind? In addition to being a scamming lowlife, he's also the worst ex-boyfriend in the history of the universe considering what he put me through at the lake.

"You know I couldn't do that!" he insists through gritted teeth, taking all of my abuse.

I feel arms wrap around my midsection, but they aren't

only for me to burst forward and try to push Wesley again.

"I don't even know why you're here. I never wanted to see you again!" I call, furious.

The bouncer still has a hold of me, and I'm struggling against him, eager to give this big lug with marbles for brains a piece of my mind. Wesley has his hands up and is backing off, and I can see him locking eyes with the bouncer, who seems more concerned for Wesley's safety than mine.

"It's alright. There's no problem," he says.

But there are problems, and they're filing out of the bar to watch the commotion we made. Within the group crowding around the bar entrance and windows, I see Miles and Taylor watching to see what's going on.

First Taylor shows up, now Wesley? What's next? Is Alice going to suddenly show up with a knife still lodged in her heart?

With so many people watching, I know this is a disaster and force myself to calm down. I'm still breathing heavily and furious after being terrorized all day. I thought the creepy guy from the bar was after me, but instead it was Wesley. Seeing him here can only mean one thing. He wants something.

"Why were you sneaking around all day?" I ask, speaking low, and still at a standoff with him.

He's busy adjusting his jacket and brushing himself off.

"Because I was trying to avoid this," he says in the same tone, gesturing around at all of the people watching.

I get a sinking feeling when I realize he has a good point. I have no idea what happened to Wesley after we parted ways outside of the cabin when the geeky lunatic from the bar burst out of the woods and came after us.

I'd stupidly thought I could push Wesley in a better direction, one without lying and scamming, and a tiny part of me had been open to the thought of getting back together with him. I know better…two days later.

"So what are you doing here?" I ask.

He gives me a sidelong look and then turns to the crowd. "Show's over. There's nothing to see here, folks," he calls.

I catch eyes with Miles and Taylor, both looking relatively alarmed, but I don't for a second think that Wesley has suddenly shown up here by accident or a brilliant stroke of luck. After I reluctantly nod, they return to their seats.

It's too late to get out of this now. I'll have to hear what he came all the way from Hochatown to tell me, but after everything we went through, doing it in front of this bar with other people around is not going to work.

I glance over my shoulder at the dumpster I chucked Alice's phone into. Now that I'm less concerned about a serial killer coming after me, I turn toward the alley.

"Come with me," I say.

Wesley complies, shoving his hands in his jeans pockets and following me into the dim stretch of pavement running along behind the bar. Other than the dumpster, there are boxes and crates, empty bottles and other trash, and the smell of stale beer.

My shoes stick and make a peeling sound with every step. Hoping I've gone far enough in, I face Wesley, calm enough now to see that he also looks strung out after what happened in Hochatown. Maybe even worse than Taylor. It's his eyes. The hangdog look is something I've never seen from him before.

"Taylor told me you were here," he says.

I can't help but groan. "You've been texting with Taylor. How did you find me in the first place?"

He shrugs. "You told me where you worked. I was hoping to run into you."

"You literally did that when I was trying to leave!"

about being grabbed.

There's too much I want to understand, and I want to know it all at once, making choosing one thing difficult.

"But why?" I ask, frustrated and rubbing my eyes.

"Because you have to know what happened," he says.

That gets my attention enough to make me close my mouth. I don't know how much Taylor told him, but he might not know anything about what happened with Alice or how I've been pretending to be her all day because of the way her attempt to moonlight as an assassin backfired.

"Spill it."

I cross my arms and hope this'll be good, because there's a fair chance my time would be better off spent with Miles and Taylor trying to figure out why Bedrock Financial is suddenly starting to act like the mafia.

Wesley puts on a bitter scowl and glances my way, pausing long enough to make me actually think he's having a hard time voicing his thoughts.

"After we parted ways, I tried to get clear of the area but ended up out in the woods. I took a wrong turn somewhere and ended up wandering around for a long time. It seriously made me think I was lost. I started calling for help, hoping somebody would hear me, and eventually somebody did.

"I recognized the guy who was chasing us, except his face and chest were covered in blood. He couldn't move very well and was gasping every breath. I don't know how he didn't pass out or why he kept moving through the woods.

"He had his hand over one eye until he called back to me. When he took his hand away...gross. And now we were together, way out deep in the woods.

"I asked him what happened and what he did. For all I knew, I thought he killed you, and it burned in my stomach that I left

cabin so he could finish what he started."

My arms crossed, I watch Wesley with grim fascination as he talks about things that happened after I'd received the head injury that gave me the huge bruise on my cheek. I wondered how the guy could've been scared off by losing an eye and then recover enough to want to come back and find me again. Good thing he'd run off far into the woods and didn't simply hang around.

It makes me uncomfortable to think about how easily I could have died.

"When I told him I wasn't taking him anywhere," Wesley continues, "he got really angry. It was feral, like he was a caveman or animal. He said he was going to cut me up like the old man, that he wanted to stain the beaches red with my blood. The guy said he traveled the country picking people off.

"And the worst thing is I could see it too. He was still dressed nicely, and people would never think somebody who looked normal would do those things. Well, he didn't look normal anymore."

"What did you do?" I ask, thankful that somehow he didn't get back to me while I was still on the beach.

"Mostly I watched him, but then when he got angry, he got his hands on a rock and came after me. He was in pathetic shape, but I wasn't about to let him kill me too. I got a hold of the rock after tearing it out of his hands. He won't be bothering anybody anymore."

"You killed him?" I say reflexively, not sure if I should be horrified or relieved.

Usually when Wesley boasts, he's got a huge grin and puffs up his chest, muscles flexing. There's none of that, only a sour stare off to the side and a long face.

He can't even answer.

"He attacked me!" he says before a wave of disgust washes over him, and the next thing I know he starts choking up and hanging his head. "This is too deep, Emily. Can you imagine it? I know I've done some bad things, finding people and getting a few bucks out of them. This guy does that but kills the people. Is that what I am now because I had to get him? This is too much."

Wesley sounds different now, a yelp in his voice that I've never heard before. But it's still Wesley, and I wouldn't trust him with a Monopoly dollar. Still, I can sympathize with the feeling, which is the exact thing I've been feeling for a while.

"It was all too much," I say reflectively, staring off at the glow of the streetlight. "I'm not saying there isn't a place for fudging the truth in the world, but when I think of all the lies I've told and the hurt I've caused, I can see how little it got me."

I'm tempted to tell Wesley about Miles but think twice about it, knowing how that would go over.

"It wasn't worth it," Wesley agrees. "I should really—"

I flinch and put my hand up.

"Please save it. I can't handle another empty promise right now. I have too much to deal with, even if the guy from the bar isn't a problem anymore. At least now I'll have something to tell the sheriff's department when they get a hold of me next. Don't worry, I'll leave you out of it. But it's funny that a murder investigation ranks about fifth on my list of problems."

Wesley straightens up. He still has the hangdog look, but I can tell he's listening to me more than he usually does, and not only to wait for his turn to speak.

"What do you mean?"

I glance at him, surprised that he's giving me his full attention. My gut instinct is to keep snapping at him for stalking me today and for what he did to Cletus, but getting on his case about those things isn't going to help me now.

Wesley the truth.

"I don't know how much Taylor told you, but after you and I parted ways and before I ran into the serial killer, I met Alice in the cabin's loft. She tried to recruit me into some kind of personal servitude like Taylor, but when I said no, she and Taylor came after me and tried to kill me.

"It turns out someone at Bedrock put Alice up to it, and I've been trying to find out who and why. Somebody seems to have a personal vendetta against me, and I've spent all day trying to figure it out."

Wesley cracks a smirk, and for a second I think he's going to regress back to his juvenile ways and laugh at me, but I gradually figure out that whatever has him amused isn't me.

"Oh!" he says, arching his back and raising a hand. "I could've told you that."

My eyes widen. Is it possible Wesley actually knows something? I thought his brain was completely empty.

"How? What are you talking about?" I say, suddenly excited.

Wesley is still reeling.

"That makes so much more sense now. I've been scratching my head trying to figure out what Alice meant."

"What?"

He looks at me and sighs before spilling the beans.

"I think it was when you were off looking for your phone or something. Alice said that after you got hired, somebody very high up in the company found out and got super pissed."

I hold my breath, needing to know what Alice knew. It's possible she had a much better understanding of what the scheme against me was than Director Ron Zee let on.

"Who?" I ask. "Why?"

Wesley shrugs his thick shoulders. "She never said who, but she did say they were livid, which brought a lot of heat on to the

in charge said you were the worst mistake they ever made."

That brings a smile to my face, and I hope it's Director Zee who said that after hiring me. The wheels in my head turn with what Alice said and how it relates to Terry Glint's concern that I'm going to ruin something important.

They might've thought I was a mistake before, but they have no idea what kind of havoc I'm going to wreak now.

25

I 'm anxious to find out more now that I have more of a sense of what Alice knew was going on within the company. Did Alice hear about that from Terry Glint or someone else? I feel like I'm on the verge of a big breakthrough.

It does all assume that Wesley isn't lying, but what would he have to gain from it? I don't see him protecting the guy who chased us in the woods, and his acting isn't that good.

The bouncer gives me the stink eye when I enter Three Tequila Floor, Wesley behind me, and I promise not to jump anyone else. Miles and Taylor are at the end of the bar with the laptop out, and even from the entrance I can see they're looking at a big spreadsheet full of numbers that might make me go cross-eyed.

"Hey, that looks interesting. Have you figured anything out?" I ask, managing to draw their attention from the screen.

Taylor glances at Miles, but he has his eyes on me with a troubled look. And that's before he notices Wesley behind me.

"Who's this guy?" he asks when it becomes apparent that Wesley has come in with me and is sticking around. If I didn't know any better, I'd think Miles feels a tweak of jealousy seeing

pounds of muscle, and neat hair.

But Wesley still has his glum look, hardly paying attention. Even Taylor looks perturbed.

"Boy, Wes, you don't usually take rejection so hard. Is this the first time any girl's ever said no to you?"

He shoots her a confused look and shakes his head.

"I didn't hit on her," he says.

With Wesley being touchy and Taylor teasing him, I bizarrely feel the need to get involved after what he said.

"He's going through a lot, Taylor. Cut him some slack," I say, in disbelief that I'm defending him after everything he did.

Although in retrospect, maybe Wesley outing me as being incapable as a financial planner wasn't as consequential as it seemed considering Alice already had it in mind to kill me, even without knowing I'd lied to get my job. So why was I somebody's worst mistake?

Taylor glances at Miles, perhaps finally giving him up, and goes to Wesley's side. She wraps her arm around his.

"Is that so? I'm sure we can find a way to make it better," she says.

I sigh, still grossed out by some of their displays over the weekend, but more power to them if they can make each other happy. I only hope they can help each other be better rather than dragging each other down.

Turning back to Miles, I force a smile, like everything is peachy.

"Yeah, that's Wesley. I knew him a while back, and he joined us for a while over the weekend," I explain, leaving a lot out. "But did you find anything though?"

Miles surveys Taylor and Wesley next to each other and gives me a questioning look. I nod that it's OK. After what I've already told Wesley, there's no point hiding anything else.

at me.

"The accounting department data is helpful, but it still doesn't have anything like the Q Fund's core portfolio. Wherever the records are for the actual investments, they're being held very closely, which in a way makes sense. It's proprietary."

I cringe, some of my enthusiasm waning.

"So nothing useful?" I ask, and Miles shakes his head.

"Not at all, and what we did find from the accounting records is very confusing. With a fund of this size, you'd expect fairly massive returns in the form of interest, dividend payments, or something marking the yields of the investments, but there's really nothing like that, even though there are for some other funds."

Nodding, I try not to make it obvious that most of what he's saying is going over my head.

"Of course, that would make it different."

Miles squints at me. Oh no, I've set off his BS detector.

"Yes," he says, managing to avoid being condescending. "It means the only company revenue would be coming from service fees, which would be an unbelievably poor way to run a business like this. It's unthinkable if the investments aren't earning anything, and it would have to be showing up in these accounting records."

I optimistically glance over at Taylor, who gives me an encouraging look.

"That must be it! Somebody is mismanaging the investments! What if all of the investments are bad?"

I take a deep breath and marvel at the possibility. What if the people who started this company are as bad at investing as I am at financial planning? Maybe they're worried about me exposing them, but how would I do that? And why would they worry about me when I hardly know anything about investing?

"You're right!" he says, getting excited with me before it tapers off. "Bad investments certainly wouldn't be making much money, but that's only one possible explanation, and we can't be sure without proof. This is still not adding up for me and will require more analysis. I feel like I should have enough data but am not quite grasping it."

I nod, hopeful, even though I don't want him to turn back to the laptop when he could be giving his attention to me.

Wesley peers at the screen for a moment until his eyes glaze over.

"So who is this guy anyway, and why should we believe anything he says?" Wesley asks me, and Miles lowers his eyes.

I answer quickly, trying to reduce the tension. "This is Miles, who started at Bedrock today after graduating with a finance degree. He also thinks there are some strange things going on with the company," I say. "Now that we know who all the guys are, maybe we can refocus on figuring out what's going on. Please?"

Miles and Wesley don't look like they'll be instant best friends and keep appraising each other, leaving an opening for Taylor.

"I had no idea the company I work at is like this," she says, shaking her head. And that reminds me of what Wesley revealed in the smelly back alley.

I take a half-step closer to her and brush my hair back, trying to be friendly before broaching what is sure to be a touchy subject. We had our conversation in the bathroom about what happened, but we didn't get into this.

"Can we talk about that though? Are you absolutely sure you didn't have any idea the company is like this?"

Taylor purses her lips.

"No, I mean, everybody in the accounting department loves

was ridiculing us online, but it seems like a pretty good employer," she says, shrugging and trying to get some support from Miles, who only had one workday to go on. He looks at her skeptically.

I suck my teeth, knowing I wasn't clear enough with my question.

"Taylor, that's not what I mean exactly. Let's have a no-judgment zone for a second here, OK? You tried to stab me with a kitchen knife. When I was in the loft with Alice, she snapped her fingers, and you came after me again on command. Wesley said that she may have mentioned some things about me and people in the company being against me. What did she tell you to make you come after me? It can't all have been about your job being threatened."

Between my questions and the guys' gazes, Taylor recoils, looking uncomfortable in the spotlight. I can sympathize. It can't be that easy to have a casual conversation about that time you tried to kill the person you're talking to.

She crosses her arms and shakes her head, her ponytail flopping about.

"I think we all went a little crazy there, and I shouldn't have lost control like that. I'm sorry. As for what Alice said, her plan was to hide in the loft and come down after you when you went in, but you ended up going right up there.

"After you'd left the cabin, Alice said you needed to either join us or die, that you knew too much. She started getting into how you could cost us both our jobs, leaving us with bad references and no ability to get another job. The drinking didn't help, and I had promised her I'd do what she said, so…"

I nod haltingly, trying to fit that together with what I know. Sadly, it doesn't help much.

"So she lied her tail off and manipulated you," I say. Taylor

about people in the company who hate me, think I was a mistake, or claimed I would ruin things?"

"Truthfully, she didn't tell me much of anything about her plans. I really did think we were going to have fun," she says.

I begin to see this line of questioning being hopeless. So much for the idea that Alice let something important slip that would help me figure this out. Giving up isn't in my nature, but I start to think we've gotten all of the information we're going to get.

"At one point, Alice said something about me still being able to work at Bedrock if I agreed to her plan. Obviously that wouldn't work if she was on a mission to kill me. Do you have any thoughts about that?"

Taylor looks me in the eyes this time, giving me a flicker of hope that soon goes out.

"She probably thought she could get around the company's problem with you, making them some promise. Or she might've been blowing smoke at you."

I nod, thinking the latter was more likely. Why did I ever think Alice was trustworthy? Instead, I'm here taking the word of Taylor and Wesley, the two most notorious liars I've ever met. What a world.

I raise an eyebrow at Miles, who has a dazed look on his face after all of the killing talk. I nudge him with a finger to make sure I haven't scrambled his brain completely.

"This kind of thing didn't come up in any of my classes," he admits, and he looks so cute when he's uncomfortable.

I close my eyes for a moment, trying as hard as I can to walk myself through this, to see if I can find a way to add it up.

"I lie to get a job I'm not qualified for. Someone in management, possibly Terry Glint, finds out and says I'm a mistake. The word goes down through the HR director to Alice to get rid of me. She dies. I get her bonus check for my death. The FBI raid happens, and Glint says he and his wife are furious that I might ruin something. We become suspicious of the Q Fund."

"Is that all?" Wesley asks mockingly, and I glower at him.

"It always comes down to the same question. Why me?" I ask, raising my hands, palms up.

I look around, expecting an answer, because I sure can't figure it out.

"Maybe they think you'll kill them too," Taylor suggests, raising my hackles until I start to wonder if I would. Considering what I've been put through, they might deserve it.

"I know. They're after the junk in your trunk," Wesley says, smirking. I roll my eyes, not dignifying that with a response. I'm pretty sure this whole thing doesn't revolve around my butt. At least Wesley isn't being so mopey anymore.

Miles clears his throat, and I wonder if he has a joke too. But then he looks at me carefully, making me feel like a work of art on display.

"I think they know you're a fighter," he says.

I stifle a grin, trying not to blush while feeling deeply gratified. Proving myself and showing everyone I'm more than a girl from the streets is what I want. That's what my sister Melanie would've expected of me.

"Hoo, it's getting late," Wesley says, "and we're in a bar. We should probably be doing less talking and more drinking, right? Who's up for a round?"

I nod reluctantly, unable to imagine what else could possibly happen now that it's getting late. All of the questions remaining will have to get answered another day.

"I definitely could go for one," Taylor says, bumping Wesley with her hip.

Miles takes a last longing look at the laptop.

tomorrow after all this. I'm going to keep thinking about what this missing data means. It'll come to me."

I can relate to feeling the pressure, but at the same time letting loose for a little while seems like it would really help.

"I'm in!" I say.

Wesley chuckles. "My treat. I promise it's my money."

I wonder about that while he steps up to the bar and attempts to hail the bartender. Taylor packs up her laptop, and Miles casts me an awkward glance before looking away, making me add pondering what's on his mind to my mental queue. I thought he'd be terrified by all this and want nothing to do with me, but he's still here.

In fact, he seems more intrigued by this than he was with his work as a financial planner. Is it the sordid mess he likes, or might it be something about me?

Then I feel a hand on my arm and jerk to my right, finding Shaylene the server with a ghostly look on her already pale face.

She manages to pull me a couple of steps away and then whispers into my ear.

"That's him with the black jacket, isn't it? Your stalker? Don't worry. I've already called the police. They'll be here any second."

I look at her to see if she's serious.

Now all the blood drains from my face.

Oh no.

26

"Shaylene, you've got it all wrong. No, no, no!" I say, jerking my head to the bar's front entrance, where I don't see anything but the black of night.

I don't know how much time we have, but it can't be much. We'll never find out what's going on if we're tied up with the police.

"I get it. He might hear you. Act natural. Help is on the way, Alice," Shaylene says with a wink as my heart rate skyrockets.

I keep shaking my head, suddenly nervous. I want to tell her again that she's got it all wrong, that Wesley isn't the guy I thought was after me. I can't bring myself to call him a good guy, but it's possible he's finally realizing the error of his ways.

There's no time for any of that, but I do need to say one thing to Shaylene. I grab hold of her sleeve and position my head right in front of hers to look her dead in the eyes.

"My name is Emily!"

She stares blankly at me, but I'm already backing away. Arguing with her is a lost cause since the damage is done and the police are on their way. They would have a field day consid-

out of.

I turn quickly to the others, panicked.

"We have to get out of here now! The police are coming!"

Miles, Wesley, and Taylor stare at me, the hamster wheels turning in their heads. None of them move, and I twitch, gesturing for them to get moving.

Wesley and Taylor glance at each other and then burst out laughing, Taylor leaning against him to keep her balance.

"That's hysterical, Emily. The cops are coming! Ahh! I've been waiting all night for your jokes," she says, chuckling.

I shake my head hard.

"I'm not kidding. The server called the cops. She thinks Wesley's suspicious."

Wesley scratches his chin then breaks into a broad grin.

"She's right. Ask any girl in here. I'm top of the list for Dallas's most wanted," he brags, scratching the back of his head as an excuse to flex his bicep.

Miles cringes at them.

"I think she's serious," he says.

I'm already backing away. Even what I did in the Bedrock human resources office would mean jail time, not to mention pulling the fire alarm or everything in Hochatown.

Smirking, Taylor rolls her eyes at Miles.

"You have to know when she's being a drama queen. She likes to invent these emergencies, like when she lost her phone," she says, and I'm ready to pull my hair out.

"My phone actually got destroyed!" I remind her. "We are running out of time!"

Wesley sighs.

"Alright, sheesh, you could've just said you wanted to get going," he says, raising a finger. "Let me down my beer before we

me moving."

I feel like I'm going to scream and contemplate ditching them to save myself, but then I look over my shoulder and see the lights flashing against the entryway and the front windows. Looking back, I see that their expressions have changed.

Gone are the carefree smirks and smiles. Now all three of them are staring in the direction I was. Even over the noise of the bar, we can hear vehicles approaching.

Taylor is the first to move.

"Why didn't you say something, Emily?"

Groaning, I start hustling with them, but we quickly realize that the front entryway would only put us in their waiting arms. We instead turn to the side entrance, and in only a couple of steps I look back and see the squad cars pulling in to a stop and unloading some of Dallas's finest.

"The side door," Miles suggests as we weave through the crowd, but that would only put us out onto the side street, not far away from the intersection.

I can't blame Miles for not having the kind of experience I do that would allow him to think farther outside the box.

"No, the kitchen," I say, banking on a back exit being our best chance of getting away unseen.

We leave the bar area behind. Wesley's new tab is unpaid, but that's what happens when you call the cops on your patrons. One after the other, we trot single file around the seating area and reach the bar's rear, pushing open the swinging door near the bathrooms and enter the kitchen.

Shaylene is there, looking shocked as we barge in and start rushing across the tile floor between the sinks and the fryers. A couple of Hispanic cooks start calling to us in Spanish, but we're not about to stop for anything.

A rear exit is straight ahead, and I shoulder open the door

around at where we are and what options we have. The first thing I notice is that Wesley sticky-fingered some chicken fingers on his way through the kitchen and is now munching on them.

I realize we're at the end of the small alley with the dumpster.

"Where now?" Miles asks, seemingly expecting me to have a plan. He looks far less comfortable now, his eyes wide and breathing heavily like he's in the middle of a race.

I don't have the heart to tell him I don't know, and I realize that this alley runs an L-shape along each side of the building all the way to the street on both sides. There are no adjoining alleyways, ladders, cellar doors, or other ways out. A few second-story windows on other buildings aren't accessible.

It's one side or the other, and all I can do is decide based on the flashing red and blue lights shining brighter on the side where Wesley and I had conversed by the dumpsters.

"This way," I say, gesturing in the opposite direction, my confidence slipping.

If we can get out onto the street and get some distance, we might be alright. We start running the length of the alley.

When we're about halfway, another police car pulls right up, its tail end blocking the alley's exit. It's enough to bring us to a halt, and we begin slowly backtracking.

My body's aches and pains have been replaced by a tingling sensation in my fingers, my nerves ratcheting up. We're all breathing hard now but are running out of options.

As the officers' shadows start to loom at the end of the alley, we creep back toward the corner.

"I've never said a word to a police officer in my life," Miles says nervously, making my head snap in his direction. His jaw is quivering, even though as best I can tell he's never done

us for one night.

It's hard for me to stay focused when he makes an admission like that. Living on the streets of Dallas since I was eighteen, police encounters have been a part of daily life.

"They're going to fingerprint me," Taylor says, terrified in a way I've never seen her before.

That would put her front and center for Alice's murder investigation, a lifetime behind bars for being Alice's unwitting accomplice to the planned Bedrock hit job against me.

"Emily, we have to get out of here," Wesley says.

The look in his eyes that I saw in the alley the last time we were here is back. But it's not only vulnerability. It's fear. He doesn't have to say anything more for me to understand what he's facing. Once the police get their hands on him, he'll get pinned for everything he's ever done.

Should Wesley face the consequences for all of his bad actions? Probably. But it looks like he might actually be turning onto a better path, and I want to see where it goes. That'll never happen if he's suddenly locked up.

As for me, I suppose I should be breathing easy here. I'm the stalking victim Shaylene called the police to protect, right? But I don't think I'll be able to figure out what's going on with this company contract to kill me on my own. I need their help.

We back farther into the corner, police slowly creeping our way from both sides. Their guns aren't drawn, and there hasn't even been any shouting. That's how confident they are that they have us.

"We need to think of something to tell them," I say, struggling to figure out what to do.

"A scam," Wesley says, nodding slightly.

He draws a look from Miles. A lightbulb seems to go off in his head. "A scam... Wait a minute."

hasn't come up with anything helpful, I'm disappointed but can't dwell on it. Taylor is huddling in the middle of us, making it clear she's not going to pull a rabbit out of a hat that gets us out of this either.

No, it's up to me to find a way to get the police off our backs and get out of here.

"We could tell them it's a mistake. They're looking for other people who look like us. The server hates us and called the cops as a prank. We could try to bribe them. If we stay still like mannequins, they might walk right by us."

I babble until Miles puts his hand on my shoulder. Glancing over at him, I see him shaking his head, shutting down all of my terrible ideas.

No, it's too late for any of that. The only thing that's left is for us to face the music. Well, not all of us. Miles and I will be fine, but Taylor and Wesley will probably be doing hard time until their hair is gray.

"What if I fake being pregnant?" Taylor asks. "Morning sickness."

"It's nighttime," Wesley says.

The cops keep closing in, our time running out. I can see the mustaches from here even in the dim light.

I gasp, hitting on something.

"What if we tell them the truth? Bedrock, a massive financial institution, has organized a failed attempt to kill me because they're covering up some kind of impropriety with their Q Fund."

"They'll never believe it," Wesley says.

I'm tempted to pull out the ten-thousand-dollar check, which has to count as proof, but Miles slips into another one of his mental trances.

"It's a scam, but how? What if it's all a scam?" he wonders,

Thinker statue.

Suddenly the door to the kitchen bursts open in front of us, revealing a large police officer with a mustache, beady eyes, and a stomach looking like he's smuggling a bowling ball in it. The bright kitchen lights shine around him, casting him in stark relief.

Wesley and Taylor shrink back to the bricks walls behind us. Swallowing my trepidation, I step forward.

"I'm sorry, Officer, but there's been a mistake! This man isn't stalking me. He's my friend. I just didn't realize who he was at first. I think that server is a little off, if you know what I mean," I plead as the officer lumbers down the steps.

He stops in front of me, looming about a foot taller than I am, and looks over me to Miles, Taylor, and Wesley behind me. He peers hard at them before turning his attention to me, raising my hopes that he'll accept my story, which really is the truth. Miles should be proud. Not one lie.

"What's your name?" he asks, putting me on the spot.

"Emily Marks," I say, ready for the sympathetic response and the whole thing to be called off.

"Right."

In a flash, the officer reaches out and snatches my wrist, pulling me close enough to him to whiff a weird mix of after-shave and coffee. My eyes widen as I feel his grip.

"Wait, what are you doing?" I ask, struggling.

Why is he doing this to me when I'm the victim? I start to moan as I try to free myself, but there's no way I'm getting away from him.

"The rest of you are free to go," the officer says in his thick baritone voice before lowering his gaze to me. "As for you, Emily Marks, you are under arrest for possession of a fake driver's

will be used against you..."

Too blindsided to continue to struggle, I gape at the officer as he spins me around and cuffs my hands together behind my back.

All I can do is stare at Taylor, Wesley, and Miles as they gape back at me.

That Shaylene is such a little liar.

My eyes well up as the officer continues to recite my rights. A Class A misdemeanor, seriously? That's a fine of thousands of dollars and a year in jail, and who knows how much more when they figure out what I've done.

"Please, no," I mutter, distraught, but the officer doesn't listen to my pleas. He doesn't care that people are trying to kill me and that I have to figure out what's going on at Bedrock, why someone at the top of the company is out to get me.

The other police officers have arrived from the alleyways and begin shooing the others away. As relieved as I'm sure they are, Taylor and Wesley at least look sympathetically at me as they quickly comply.

Miles does one better. When the big officer starts to tug me away backward, Miles steps up to me and leans in, pressing his lips to mine. The kiss only lasts for a moment, and as much as I want to savor it, it's another heartbreaking reminder of what I stand to lose.

How many more kisses would we have if I don't spend the next year in jail?

We're torn apart by the officer's pulling, and some other offi-

in the other direction.

"Miles!" I wail, losing my composure again for the second time today.

He's reaching out for me in the midst of the confusion and voices, his garbled voice calling out right before I lose sight of him, "Emily, it's Ron Zee's scheme!"

"What?" I yell. "What about Ron Zee?"

From the desperate look in his eyes, I see that something had occurred to him at the last possible moment before he was pulled out of view.

Human Resources Director Ron Zee? Why would it be his scheme? What could Miles have figured out that would make him the one responsible for trying to kill me? Director Zee is far below Vice President Terry Glint, and Alice had said someone at the top thought I was their biggest mistake.

It's not adding up, but all I can do is feel my head spin as I'm jerked and tugged at the direction of the police officer. When my heels hit upon a hard surface, nearly tripping me as I'm taking a step backward, a firmer realization hits me.

He's taking me back through the bar.

Petrified and dying of embarrassment, I taste my salty tears when I swallow. He drags me up the stairs and through the door.

The officer hauls me in front of him so that he can prod me onward through the kitchen from behind. The cooks stare blankly at me, and this is only the first taste of my walk of shame. When we pass out of the kitchen into the barroom, the reaction is pulverizing.

There have to be fifty to eighty people here, and they all gawk at me, all other movement ceasing while the music still plays. Of all the musicians in the world, it's Beyoncé. Why'd she have to make a country music album?

After only a few steps, the laughter starts, then the jeers,

eyes, but I can't brush it forward with my hands cuffed behind my back. I can't help but glance around, spotting the table where we'd had our girls' night, now occupied by other people, the bartender cringing at me oddly, and a grinning guy I don't know trying to snap a selfie with me.

And then I spot Shaylene along the end of the bar, arms crossed and a smirk stretching across her face. Her freckles and red hair catch the overhead lights. Of course she's right there, and I have to march past her.

"Crybaby!" she heckles me, and I'm overcome with revulsion.

So much for my attempt to show some vulnerability with her in the bathroom. After Hochatown, I should've learned my lesson that any attempt to get anyone on my side will always backfire.

I take a sudden step in her direction, stomping hard and coming to a halt right in front of her. Shaylene flinches, putting her hands up, and I find enough enjoyment in her panicked reaction to smile.

"Try not to spill any more beer," I say quickly.

"Get moving!" the officer says behind me, forcing me past her.

My momentary reprieve from the humiliation is over, and it's back to marching on toward the front entrance, where the police cruisers still have their lights flashing.

Now I'm smart enough to put my head down, eyes on the floor. I can't bear to see another person mocking me or taking pictures of me to put on the internet. I'm probably going to be the laughingstock of Dallas for the rest of my life.

The cooler air outside hits me, and I glance up to see the bouncer give the police officer a nod and half-smile. Then his eyes settle on me, seeing me for the troublemaker I am after the

deserved it for lurking around me all day.

The police cruiser is a few steps away, and one of the other officers is holding a rear door open for me. I wish I'd thought to throw Alice's card wallet into the dumpster when I'd tossed her phone, but now I'm going to have no defense against the charges. No lawyer. No hope.

There are more people outside, not only bar patrons but people simply walking around the neighborhood. I've never felt this low. Of all the things I could've ever been caught and arrested for, this seems so petty. It feels like tripping over my shoelaces compared to the terrible, illegal things I've done.

The officer's hand palms my skull as he guides me into the backseat of the squad car. He closes the door so fast that it catches me on the butt, making me spill forward against the seat, struggling to right myself without the use of my hands. The black upholstery is not nearly as soft as it looks.

Eventually I manage to sit up and look out the window, the last of my freedom officially gone.

Next I expect the officer to get in the front seat and drive me to the station, but for some reason they don't seem in a rush about it. From where I am, it's hard to see what the officers are doing—standing around talking to someone, I believe.

If they're going to take my life away, I wish they'd hurry up and do it, but instead they keep taking their sweet time talking to someone in a navy jacket. Probably a detective or something. I can't see his face or much of him at all between the officers.

I have nothing else to do but think, and my thoughts return to what Miles said. Ron Zee? Why on Earth would he think Ron Zee, the director whose office I ransacked, was behind everything?

Racking my brain to picture the moment, I start to shake my head. No, he didn't say "Ron Zee's scheme." It was something

take me out. I misheard him in the commotion.

The cruiser door opens, but it's not the front door. It's the back door that I'd entered through, and for some reason the big officer is looking in at me with an even sourer look on his face than he had before.

"Get out," he says.

As much as I'd love to get out of this police car, I'm skeptical about what this means. Considering some of the things I've heard about encounters with police, I don't know what they could have in store for me outside of the vehicle.

"What? Why?" I ask.

The officer's mustache twitches.

"I didn't tell you to talk. I told you to get out," he says.

Since we're still right in front of Three Tequila Floor, I hope nothing too bad could possibly happen to me out here, though I might again be in view of more people. Reluctantly, I scoot to the edge of the seat and start to climb out.

It's a struggle. Everything would be so much easier if my hands weren't cuffed behind my back. It's almost like the police want to prevent me from using my body.

I set one foot on the pavement and then the other, standing up and squinting in the glare of the bar lights and streetlight. It takes me a second to get my bearings and notice what's around me.

That's when I see who they're talking to.

Staring right at me are the two FBI agents.

28

The taller one, a hot bad boy with tattoos on his neck, gives me a smoldering look. The shorter one with the thick arms and broken nose who'd interrogated me is lecturing the police officers.

A shiver passes over me, and this time it's not from the breeze. I don't know what I was afraid of when the officer told me to get out of the car, but this seems much worse.

"What's happening?" I ask, and the shorter agent immediately breaks away from the Dallas PD officers, giving me an icy glare.

"You're coming with us," he says.

I gasp at the prospect of facing everything they know about me, everything I stupidly admitted to in that interrogation. Inching back, I turn desperately to the big officer who'd cuffed me.

"No, you can't do this. You're the one who arrested me for the fake ID charge. I admit to everything. I did it!" I say, trying to keep my voice from warbling.

The officer doesn't even bother to look at me, this time popping the front door of his cruiser open.

as he plunks into the driver's seat.

The bulldog FBI agent takes me by the arm, yanking me away from the curb. It only takes moments for the police cruisers to pull away, leaving me with the pair of agents. The tall one's constant hungry gazes become sickening but not unexpected. He seemed like a seedy creep hidden in an FBI jacket the first time I saw him in the hall.

"Alright, let's get out of here," the shorter agent, presumably the one in charge, says to the other.

They each take one of my arms and start guiding me forward. Any thought of them taking these cuffs off has vanished. Unless the officer thought to give one of them the key, I might be wearing these things for a long time.

We only make it a couple of steps when I see someone among the dozen or so by the bar still watching what happens to me.

Beer in hand and a big smile on her face, it's Shelley, standing there and relishing every minute of my unfortunate experience getting manhandled on the street. It looks like she found an excuse to avoid her deadbeat husband a little longer.

Unlike with Shaylene, when I charge at Shelley, I'm not faking it. I'm ready to plow right into her, knock her over, and stomp her to pieces, but the agents catch me and prevent me from getting to her.

She laughs while I'm squirming and foaming.

"Nice working with you, Emily!" she says.

I grit my teeth and growl. She knew. Maybe she didn't know it was me all day, but she knew something about the company trying to get me and was maybe even involved. She must've called someone and tipped them off that I was here, making sure the FBI agents got me.

It only makes me angrier, but the pair of agents start

Bedrock building.

Soon enough, Shelley and the rest of the bar are out of sight, and all I can do is seethe at being ratted out, arrested, tossed around, ratted out again, and now marched off along the dark street.

"Where are you guys taking me?" I ask.

Instead of answering me, they look at each other.

"Do you think this'll make up for it?" the tall one asks the stout, short one, who shrugs.

"We can hope. Not a minute too soon. She's blown her top."

I shake my head, fuming, but it turns out I don't need them to answer. My destination becomes clear enough when I start to make out the black SUV parked in front of the Bedrock building. From there, I can only guess where they'll take me, what I'll be charged with, or what my life will become.

But I'm confident that nothing will ever be the same again.

Maybe it's the nerves, but I'm feeling chatty. If I could get this guy to talk before, I might be able to do it again. I feel like I have minutes before I'm locked into their system with no hope of ever getting out.

"Who is 'she?' The FBI director?"

When they look at each other, this time I glance at the taller one, whose collar is riding down a bit more than earlier while he walks, revealing more of his neck tattoo. I'm still not able to see all of it or recognize what it is, but it makes me think of a gang symbol.

The shorter agent chuckles.

"You could say that," he says, which seems like a strange response. Why wouldn't he simply say yes if she was?

"Who is she?"

"You don't need to worry yourself about that," he says.

When I see him smile at me, I notice he's missing a tooth.

the feeling that the FBI is hiring some awfully rough dudes these days. These agents are more thuggish than anything. Maybe they're ex-military, but from the way they walk and their voices, these guys strike me as having seen and done some awful things.

Their seedy manner makes my confidence start to slip enough to try resorting to some desperate measures.

"There's got to be a way we can call it even right now," I say, unable to keep the trepidation out of my voice. If these guys are that rough around the edges, I wonder if a deal is possible, though I'm worried about what kind of deal the tall one giving me the lurid looks would want.

He does give me a look and opens his mouth, but before he can say anything, the shorter one nudges me forward almost hard enough to make me trip. I struggle to keep my balance, the accumulated injuries in my ankle, leg, and hip flaring up.

"I don't think so. There's no way you're getting out of this one, Emily," he says, making me jerk my head in his direction.

How does he know my real name? Shelley? Somehow he figured it out since our discussion in the room with no window. I'd told them I wasn't Alice, but he never even asked me my real name. I should've known something was up then.

The black SUV is right ahead, though I can't see any other agents around. Maybe these two are the only ones putting in the overtime to get me back.

I start to drag my feet, shuffling enough to make them push me onward. All I know is I don't want to get into that SUV.

"Please," I say, "all that stuff I told you before. It wasn't true. I don't have any suspicions about Bedrock. Everything was an accident. I promise!"

Miles would not be proud of me for lying, but at this point

on the FBI agents than it did with the police officer.

We're right at the vehicle, which is all set to drive me somewhere I'll never come back from. The streetlight glints off the side, but the tinted windows prevent me from seeing anything inside. There could be a dozen more guys within.

"Save it!" the short one snaps in his raspy voice, seemingly tired of my talking.

He gives me another shove, but it's not in the direction of the van.

Staggering, I manage to keep my feet under me while realizing that they're now pushing me to the right in the direction of the Bedrock building's front door.

Wait, what? Why wouldn't they be taking me away to wherever the FBI offices and holding cells are? I jerk back and forth, trying to find any kind of sign as we move closer and closer to the building's dark doors.

But all I can see is the weird and completely unprofessional neck tattoo and the other guy's grizzled appearance and broken nose. They're wearing navy-blue jackets with "FBI" emblazoned in big yellow letters on the back, but I blink hard at the only reasonable conclusion. This settles it.

These guys aren't with the FBI.

29

B racing my feet against the sidewalk as best I can, I refuse to move forward and enter this building. The two thugs with FBI jackets push me forward, but I twist and jerk and stomp, doing everything I can to get away.

There's no way I'm going back into that building, where somebody working there has been trying to kill me for reasons I still don't know.

Gasping and screeching, I start to call for help when a hard shove sends me flying right into the hard glass door. I smack my forehead and groan.

The next thing I know, the door opens enough for them to drag me through into the darkened space inside.

It's mind-boggling trying to figure out what is going on and what this means. If these guys aren't FBI agents, who are they? Who are they working for? Why are they bringing me back here?

But that's only the tip of the iceberg. What was that whole FBI raid about? What were these guys doing here asking around about an unauthorized transaction when they aren't even part of the FBI?

which would be why they're bringing me back inside. But why would a company send fake FBI agents into the company's offices to run amok under the guise of an investigation?

My mind spins, unable to figure any of it out. It makes no sense whatsoever. But then I arrive at the question that always trips me up.

What does any of this have to do with me? I'm a young woman trying to make something of my life after a miserable childhood and being on the streets since I was eighteen years old. All I wanted was a good job. Why try to kill me for it and send fake FBI officers after me?

I still don't have my feet under me, and my arms start to ache from the two guys dragging me across the large lobby floor. There are only some minimal security lights on but no actual security that might help me. We're heading in the direction of the elevators, and I'm helpless to resist.

"Who do you work for?" I ask, coughing.

They snicker.

"Oh, she's a smart one," they say to each other, although they wouldn't say that if they knew how little I understand about any of this.

"Is it Terry Glint?"

The laughter stops, making me think I've got the right answer, although of course this vice president of the company is certainly not the "she" they were referring to earlier. Is this woman the one behind everything?

I venture a guess. "Is it his wife?"

The conversation I overheard while in the ceiling comes back to me, Glint's furious wife who was concerned that I would ruin everything.

What exactly is there to ruin? A fake FBI investigation? An attempt to kill me?

"Get in there," the shorter one says viciously. They throw me inside the elevator, flinging me like a rag doll, and I land hard on my shoulder, unable to move. The two men step inside with me, and the door closes. Tilting my head a little, I can see them push the button for the eighth floor, the top floor.

It strikes me that the eighth floor is where I'll be killed, where the hit job Bedrock has been running against me will finally without fail come to a close. I've never even heard of anyone going to the eighth floor.

Struggling to get up, I roll onto my knees while the elevator doors close. Bringing one foot up hurts, but I force myself to stand, half expecting the two men to knock me down again. Instead, they stand there with hands held in front of themselves, almost as if they were real FBI agents.

"Why were you investigating an unauthorized transaction when you're not even part of the FBI?" I ask.

Other than some uncomfortable ogling from the tall one, there's no response. The elevator starts to move, and it's almost enough to make me lose my balance.

Now that they've come this far, they don't seem to have any interest in engaging with me. I need to figure this out for myself. I want to find a way out of this. I have to survive. And there are only a few minutes left for me to do so.

Breathing deeply and shutting my eyes, I try to think even though I have an awful headache and the elevator is humming.

"What is going on with the Q Fund? Is someone stealing the dividends? Are the investments shady?" I remember my idea from earlier. "Has the fund been mismanaged? Is it about to lose a lot of money?"

The two men act like I'm not even there, and I realize I'm talking to myself. That's fine, because I have a sense that I'm closing in on something, if I could only grasp it. These two guys

doubtful they know much of anything besides who pays them and what they're supposed to do.

"What is the connection between me and the Q Fund?" I ask, looking hard at the shorter one, who cracks a smirk, but it's more at my frustration than because he has any idea about the answer. "I've never invested in anything in my life. I have no money. Math is not my forte. Agh, I wish I could figure this out!"

Beating myself over the head won't help, and I turn away from them in disgust to look at my reflection in the elevator doors. I'm beat up, dirty in a stained undershirt, and the bruise on my face is reappearing.

"Why are they so afraid that I'll ruin it? Why me?"

I look into my face, my eyes. Brushing my dirty-blonde hair away, I think I have so little power, no influence whatsoever outside of this body of mine, but someone on the eighth floor feels differently. Like Miles said, they're afraid I'm capable of much more than it appears, and that's what I have to remember.

The elevator keeps pinging as we rise up the building floor after floor. There isn't much time left, and I feel like I've gotten nowhere with my thinking. The light on the display keeps shifting to the right, and the eighth floor is getting so close.

We must be nearing the hive mind of this whole place. I imagine the real eggheads are up here engineering everything, playing all of us down below like puppets on strings. Miles was on to something, and the closest I've come to an answer is the thing he shouted that I couldn't hear correctly.

I shake my head, hitting on something. For most of the day, Miles wasn't aware of the plot to kill me, and even afterward he focused on the financial misconduct. That's what he must've figured out.

Taking a deep breath, I feel like I'm a step closer.

"It's not Ron Zee's scheme, but it sounds like it. Maybe he

it. He figured out what it is!"

Is this turning into a game of charades?

The elevator dings again, and this time the doors part in front of me, revealing a plush carpet, fancy chandelier, and a round table in the center of the room featuring an elaborate marble statue of the Bedrock logo, a big B partially carved out of rock.

This place looks more like a swanky hotel lobby rather than an office building, and the two agents break from their positions in the back of the elevator to force me into it. Now they've got me by the elbows again, guiding me along.

I can barely think, let alone breathe, and what I really want to do is stare at the molded wooden walls and ceiling, everything pristine and glistening under the overhead lights.

So much money went into these finishes and not into the investments.

I gasp, coming to a stop until they push me onward. As much as I enjoyed thinking out loud, even this one seems too galling to speak.

It's not Ron Zee's scheme. It's a Ponzi scheme!

I'm so absorbed in my thoughts that I barely realize I'm walking through the hall, which has so few doors or windows, but I do spot an open door to a bathroom and then what looks like a kitchen down a hall. If I didn't know better, I would say that someone lives up here.

And whoever is up here has been perpetrating a massive fraud that goes to the heart of the company. The Q Fund is a scam. It's all fake. There are no investments. All of the old ladies, like the one who visited Miles earlier, are dumping money into a singular company account that according to the accounting department has no records and no reporting.

barely stand up.

"So that's what you guys are doing here," I say, not bothering to fill them in on what even they don't know.

This whole fake FBI raid is a cover-up. No one's going to ask questions or think anything's wrong if they think the FBI has gone through everything with a fine-toothed comb.

But who would do such a thing? How could someone build such a massive empire that's rotten to the core?

We reach the end of the hall, where we come to an office door. The answer is staring right at me in decorative lettering on the semi-opaque glass. Chief Executive Officer Candace Roberts.

I only have a second to squint as the fake agents continue to shunt me toward the door of the CEO of this fake company. Candace Roberts? I've heard the name, but I have no idea who she is. I've never spoken to her or seen her. And I'm again left wondering what this all has to do with me.

Yes, I've figured out what they're doing, but I sure never would have if they hadn't come after me so hard. Whatever kind of scary monster I am, it's entirely of their own making. If hiring me was their biggest mistake, they kept making plenty more afterward.

The shorter thug reaches out to twist the gold knob on the CEO's office door, which swings open without the slightest squeak.

If I thought the hallway was rich, this office is decadent to a degree that is difficult to comprehend. Besides the bookshelves, the leather chairs, the regal mahogany desk with the high-backed black chair behind it, there are floor-to-ceiling windows with a miraculously gorgeous view of downtown Dallas and the city lights at night.

A top-of-the-line computer, famous artwork on the walls,

trove beyond anything I could imagine. And it all came from a scam of breathtaking size—fraud and theft, plain and simple.

The two goons take their positions on either side of the door, much like they did in the elevator, leaving me to slowly inch across the spacious office. I sense that there is someone in the chair looking out the windows, Candace Roberts if the name on the door is anything to go by.

But I'm about halfway across the large room, at a loss for what I should say or do or how I should deal with the horrible things going on with this company, when the chair starts to spin.

I don't know what Candace Roberts is supposed to look like, and I may never know, because the woman I see seated in the chair certainly isn't her, if she even exists.

But I can tell exactly how this lady looks, since she's sitting right in front of me, and I recognize her instantly.

It's my mom.

30

I gasp at the sight of Diedre Marks, her hair dark-blonde like mine but with little wingtips that would be considered retro. It's been over five years since I last saw her, which was when she went away to prison after the fraud court case, and in that time I can see some age lines have set in around her eyes and mouth.

But she has oven ten years left on her prison sentence with Dad, so how could she be here at the top of this company?

Her scowl carries plenty of disdain.

"That aghast look, is this any way to greet your mother, Emily?"

I blink and am tempted to rub my eyes, having trouble believing what I'm seeing. She makes no move to step away from her desk, merely standing there with her fingertips against the surface, looking at me with the judgmental look I know so well. She's got a slender figure and has been keeping in good shape, which is apparent even in a long-sleeve button-up white blouse and black skirt.

She looks like a professional, even if I know she's not.

"Mom? What are you doing here? What's going on?" I ask, my voice not sounding like my own.

head, already exasperated with the conversation and casting her blue eyes at the ceiling.

"Why are you asking questions you already know the answer to? Didn't I teach you better than that?" she grumbles.

Although she didn't teach me better than anything, she is right that I don't have to pretend like I don't know anything. After going through so much, I've found out a lot that I can be confident in.

"You're running an investment company that doesn't make any investments. You're the CEO under a fake name. You live up here to avoid anyone seeing you or finding out who you are. And today you've run a phony FBI investigation to terrorize the staff. Most of them are wretched monsters anyway," I say.

That gets a wan smile out of her, but then her gaze shifts to the two men by the door.

"You can both get ready for departure," she says before sauntering around the desk to my side so she can lean against its edge while facing me. "Pretty good. Is that everything?"

While noticing her bare calves and the nice flats she's wearing, I hear the men slip out the door behind me. It clicks closed lightly, leaving me alone with someone I didn't think I'd be seeing again for a good ten years when she'd be solidly in her fifties.

I wanted my family to be together again, but not like this.

"When you found out that I joined the company, you tried to get rid of me. First you told Terry Glint, who told Ron Zee, who told Alice Patterson, who attempted to kill me last weekend in Hochatown. Do you know that Alice is dead because of what you did?" I say.

Mom clicks her tongue, nodding lightly and very clearly unconcerned with the news I'm sharing. She glances at a sparkly watch on her wrist.

mutters absently before giving me another look that turns into a cringe as she notices more about my disheveled state. "And why did I do that?"

Now I give her a sour look, not exactly getting the point of this conversation. She always told me to keep my mouth shut, but I'm angry at being put through all of this and want her to know what I know. There's no way she's getting away with what she's done.

"Because you're afraid that I'll expose you and that you'll be held responsible," I say, sensing the door reopening behind me, but I don't turn even as a figure strolls into the room. "You're afraid that hiring me was your biggest mistake."

Someone walks in, a man in a dark-gray suit brushing by me, and he immediately draws Mom's attention. I quickly recognize the salt-and-pepper hair, the few extra inches of height, and the smell of bourbon that I haven't smelled in years but recognize instantly. My eyes widen.

"Did you hear that? She thinks hiring her was our biggest mistake."

The man chuckles, continuing toward her.

"We have to get going," he says, his voice scratchier than I remember it.

It's Terry Glint, but it's definitely not Terry Glint.

"I know," she says.

One hand in his pocket, he walks right up to Mom and leans against her, kissing her on the lips. It keeps going, turning into an open-mouthed kiss with a lot of tongue, the kind of lip-locking you'd expect from teenagers.

And I have to stand there and watch my parents make out until they slowly disengage, Marty Marks with a smug grin, apparently reveling in his freedom. My mom appears to have perked up as well, not that it'll do me any good.

because they've been running this scam together. They're on the cusp of making a getaway now that the FBI raid will provide them cover for some time. And once the smoke clears and somebody does realize that they've cleaned out the company, they'll be long gone.

My dad eventually gets around to casting me a scornful glance, like I'm something the cat dragged in.

"I'm afraid our mistake started way before you ever set foot in Bedrock," he says, his voice a little different than I remember it. These past few years appear to have been good to him too. Though the gray has snuck into his hair, he appears fitter than I remember, perhaps having lost a few pounds. He was always known for his charming smile and easy manner, while my mom was the visionary plotter.

"Yeah, when?" I say.

A devilish grin appears on Mom's face, and she bites her lip a little before blurting out, "How about the day you were born? Gosh, I've wanted to say that for so long."

She tosses her head back, like she's indulging in a guilty pleasure, while it gets my hackles up.

Stupid Alice. When the higher-up said I was their biggest mistake, it was my parents, and she never could've guessed that they were talking about when they had me.

I shake my head at them subtly. I've heard a lot of horrible things from my parents, but this is new territory. And we may as well see what else has been swept under the rug now that they feel like sharing.

"Then why did you hurry up and have Melanie after I was born?" I ask, bracing myself.

Even bringing her up with them is painful after her death in a car accident in our teens, but they can't hurt me any more than

squeeze it into a ball and throw it right back.

Dad tilts his head and shrugs.

"The damage was done at that point."

Mom nods and takes over, setting a hand on the back of his neck. "No more nights together, constantly having to feed you, manage you, entertain you. You were shackles holding us back, and not a day went by when I didn't want to get away from you."

That seems generous given my recollection of their parenting style, where we often went without, whether it be stimulation, supervision, or food.

Dad gives her a smile in agreement and leans against her. They've always loved each other so much that they could never spare any for us.

I purse my lips, having patiently waited for her to finish trying to put me down.

"Yeah, such a shame my existence meant you couldn't express your heart's true desire of defrauding people as broadly and viciously as you could," I say sweetly.

Mom leers at me while Dad watches placidly, perhaps a little tipsy.

"That's harsh. Investments are inherently risky," Marty says, perhaps not knowing that I've figured everything out.

Mom gives him a hinting look, and I hurry up and pounce before I miss my chance.

"Especially risky when the money goes into your pocket and not into any kind of investment. This is the lemonade stand all over again!"

Her patience wearing thin, Mom steps away from the desk and waves the back of her hand at me.

"And you ruined that too, telling people you thought the lemonade tastes gross with so little powder in it. I could've made

me!" she howls.

I smile, feeling like it's a badge of honor. The conversation between Dad and the fake FBI agent is happening again right in front of me. A part of me should've known that someone talking about me ruining things would have to be her, but it had been too long since I'd seen her to put it together.

"And now I'm going to ruin your massive heist too. I've seen the retirees and pension fund people and hard workers who were only trying to get ahead, and you're not going to rob them blind. And you're not going to get away with trying to have me killed either."

I say it with all the confidence I can, my heart pounding in my chest as I wonder if I can get them to admit their mistake and stop before I have to make them. They turn their harsh gazes on me, but I'm not a little girl they can intimidate anymore.

"As a matter of fact, we'll get away with it fine," my dad says, lightening up as his grin returns.

"It's already too late. There's no way you can stop us. It doesn't matter what you know when you can't do anything and no one will listen to you," Mom adds condescendingly.

I grit my teeth, incensed. My breathing becomes labored, and I feel myself shaking.

Snarling, I lash back at them in the harshest way I can.

"I don't know how you got out of prison, but I'm going to send you straight back where you belong!" I call.

They glance at each other, and I'm left waiting for how they respond, sure they'll show the kind of anger and hurt that I feel and that I want them to feel too.

But instead they start laughing, uproarious, full-belly laughter that has them collapsing comfortably against each other. The noise grates against my ears, and a sinking feeling persistent chuckles.

"That's a good one, Emily. I needed that," Dad says while my mother rolls her eyes at me.

"Oh my goodness, girl. Why in heaven's name would you think we're supposed to be in prison?"

Any righteousness I felt is long gone, and once again I'm on shaky ground with no firm direction. All I can point to are these foundational things that have shaped my life, the reason I've been alone and living on the streets since age eighteen.

"But the fraud trial," I say, sputtering. "The court case, the guilty verdict, the sentencing..."

They look at me like I have three heads, and my discomfort grows. I figured out so much about what they're doing, but I never questioned this.

"Wait, you thought..." Dad says, and when the laughter starts up again, it's really at my expense.

"Emily, come on. Tell me you didn't think *we* were going to prison because of all that," Mom says acidly.

I struggle to wrap my head around this, literally able to recall the day I heard about the guilty verdict.

"But if you didn't go to prison, who did?"

Diedre Marks, with her wing-tipped hair and gentle face hiding so much underneath, squints at me like I'm the dumbest person in the world.

"Your sister."

31

"We really have to get going now, honey," Marty says to Diedre, whose eyes are fixed on me.

"Hold on. I'm not finished yet," she says, touching his arm.

Slack-jawed, I stare at my parents in disbelief that they would be so cruel as to mock my baby sister's death, acting like she's still alive. Even the mere suggestion of it is so offensive and disrespectful that it seems beneath even them.

"You're a liar!" I shout. "How can you say that about your own daughter who died just to try to hurt me?"

I'm clenching my fists, struggling to keep myself under grips. Startled, they look at me like they've forgotten that I'm here. Mom crosses her arms and lowers her eyes at me, looking like a high school English teacher who caught a student cheating.

"What nonsense is this? Liar? What, me?" she says, aggrieved. "I'm the most honest person you've ever met."

I blink. *Honest!* That was the word I've been trying to remember all day about Miles. Why couldn't I think of it? It seems like such a foreign concept. Compared to Miles, Mom is about as honest as a carnival fortune teller. Miles makes me want to be a better person. That's why I get flustered around

seem impossible.

"But we had a funeral for Melanie. Some people came. There were flowers," I say, but as I recall more, my confidence starts to wane and doubts creep in. "The casket was closed. There wasn't a priest or anyone who spoke. I don't think I ever saw an obituary."

Dad leans back and takes a deep breath like he is reliving a fond memory.

"Of course. The point was that she was dead to you. We didn't need you asking questions about why she disappeared," he says calmly, like this is a perfectly normal thing to come out of his mouth.

I clench my teeth, wondering how stupid I am and how much I've been lied to. I never saw the car accident, never saw the body or spoke to a doctor or coroner. What reason would I have to suspect this was a big trick designed solely to fool me?

And why? What was the reason for all of this? How did my sister go from not being killed in a car accident to a few years later going to prison, evidently in lieu of my parents? Where did she go?

I have trouble meeting their eyes now, not wanting to cry in front of them. I thought my own painful struggles were something to tear up over, but I succumb to a wellspring of guilt and pity that my sister might have still gone through something just as bad without me there to protect her.

"I don't believe it," I say, my voice quavering. "My sister has passed away, and you're supposed to be in prison. The last thing you said to me after the court case ended was that you were going away for a while."

Afterward, I'd gone to my aunt's for a short while, but she couldn't even take care of herself, much less a girl in her late teens, and in a snap I was on my own.

as if wondering what the mystery is about.

"Yeah, and? We said we were going away for a while...from you!"

My dad covers his mouth to hide a smirk.

"I think she made an assumption," he mutters.

The lady who gave birth to me gapes and throws her head back.

"Oh, is that it? You know, Emily, I always warned you about jumping to conclusions. I'm really not sure how we could be responsible for you imagining things like that, but you should've known better," she says, shrugging.

I feel like my head is going to cleave in two. My sister is alive but in prison. My parents are here but about to flee with their ill-gotten gains. I'm the only one standing in the way who can fix this, but I don't know how and have nothing to use against them. I can't even use my hands, because they're handcuffed behind my back.

But most of all, I don't understand why. Yes, now I know why the chief executives of the company were worried about me, because they are my parents, but why lie to me about my sister? Why abandon me to a hard life alone on the streets? Why think that the best way to resolve a conflict with me is to kill me?

I'm worried I'll never know the answers to these questions, as my parents appear increasingly agitated. My mother looks at her watch again, Dad glancing past me to the door. I'm struggling not to feel like a child, to be the grown young woman I am, but I feel so lost.

Shaking my head slightly, I know I have to keep fighting, even if all I have to defend myself with is a question.

"Why are you telling me all this?" I ask, wincing.

Exhaling audibly through her nose, Diedre looks up from her watch and regards me one more time. She runs her hand

desk.

"Because now I can have a clean conscience that I've told you the truth," she says, astoundingly managing to justify herself, "but I'm not sure how much good it'll do you. Now, we need to be on our way. Where we're going, it'll be a relief that this is one fewer thing to worry about. And where you're going...that's something for philosophers to debate."

When she reaches into her desk drawer, I assume it's for a purse or phone or something she needs to take with her, but instead she produces something dark gray and purple from her desk.

It's not until she points it at me that I realize she's holding a dainty little handgun, and my eyes widen so large it's a wonder they don't pop out of my head.

"Mom, no!"

"Goodbye, Emily!"

Mom pulls the trigger, but nothing happens, and she cringes at the weapon in her hand. While Dad rushes over, I slink back, now a good twenty feet away from her and trying to think of what else I can say. With the office door closed and my hands behind my back, I don't even think I could open it if I want to.

"You have to turn the safety off. Here, like this," Dad says helpfully, and my mother gives him a sweet look before resuming her aim.

I take another step back, shaking and feeling like my life is flashing before my eyes. For Melanie to be back only for me to be gone will burn me even in death.

"Please!" I wail, red-faced.

Diedre swallows and flexes her index finger, her eyes glazing over me with indifference like I'm nothing but a cutout target in a shooting range. Having said her goodbye, she doesn't waste

hand clenching.

She pulls the trigger, the gun fires, and I collapse to the floor.

Look for the conclusion of the Girls' Trilogy, *Girls' Time*, coming soon!

If you enjoyed *Girls' Night*, please take a moment to write a review for it. Reviews are phenomenally important and are crucial to any book's success. Thank you so much for reading and sharing your thoughts!

ABOUT THE AUTHOR

Jason Letts is the author of over thirty novels, including the bestselling *Agent Nora Wexler Mystery Series*. *Girls' Trip* and *Girls' Night* will be followed by *Girls' Time*, concluding the trilogy.

To connect and find out about more books, find me at

www.jasonletts.com

https://www.facebook.com/authorjasonletts

Or email me at infinitejuly@gmail.com

CONTENTS

COPYRIGHT & DISCLAIMER

This book is a work of fiction. Names, characters, places and incidents either are products of the author's imagination or are used fictitiously. Any resemblance to actual events or locales or persons, living or dead, is entirely coincidental.

Copyright © 2024 by Jason Letts

Made in the USA
Middletown, DE
11 August 2024

58936259R00135